CW00504543

S.A. Ferrall

A Ramble of Six Thousand Miles Through the United States of America

S.A. Ferrall

A Ramble of Six Thousand Miles Through the United States of America

1st Edition | ISBN: 978-3-75236-032-5

Place of Publication: Frankfurt am Main, Germany

Year of Publication: 2020

Outlook Verlag GmbH, Germany.

A RAMBLE OF SIX THOUSAND MILES THROUGH THE UNITED STATES OF AMERICA.

BY S. A. FERRALL

PREFACE.

The few sketches contained in this small volume were not originally intended for publication—they were written solely for the amusement of my immediate acquaintances, and were forwarded to Europe in the shape of letters. Subsequent considerations have induced me to publish them; and if they be found to contain remarks on some subjects, which other travellers in America have passed over unnoticed, the end that I have in view will be fully answered.

Although I remained in the seaboard cities sufficiently long to have collected much information; yet knowing that the statistics of those places had been so often and so ably set before the public, I felt no inclination to trouble my friends with their repetition.

In Europe, the name of America is so associated with the idea of emigration, that to announce an intention of crossing the Atlantic, rouses the interfering propensity of friends and acquaintances, and produces such a torrent of queries and remonstrances, as will require a considerable share of moral courage to listen to and resist. All are on the tiptoe of expectation, to hear what the inducements can possibly be for travelling in America. America!! every one exclaims—what can you possibly see there? A country like America—little better than a mere forest—the inhabitants notoriously far behind Europeans in refinement—filled with wild Indians, rattle-snakes, bears, and backwoodsmen; ferocious hogs and ugly negros; and every other species of noxious and terrific animal!

Without, however, any definite scientific object, or indeed any motive much more important than a love of novelty, I determined on visiting America; within whose wide extent all the elements of society, civilized and uncivilized, were to be found—where the great city could be traced to the infant town—where villages dwindle into scattered farms—and these to the log-house of the solitary backwoodsman, and the temporary wig-wam of the wandering Pawnee.

I have refrained nearly altogether from touching on the domestic habits and manners of the Americans, because they have been treated of by Captain Hall and others; and as the Americans always allowed me to act as I thought proper, and even to laugh at such of their habits as I thought singular, I am by no means inclined to take exception to them.

CHAPTER I

Following the plan I had laid down for myself, I sought and found a goodly Yankee merchantman, bound for and belonging to the city of New York. Our vessel was manned with a real *American* crew, that is, a crew, of which scarcely two men are of the same nation—which conveys a tolerably correct notion of the population of the United States. The crew consisted of one Russian, one German, one Italian, one Scotchman, one Newfoundlander, one Irishman, two Englishmen, two New Englanders, and two Negros—the cook and steward. The seamen of America are better paid, and better protected, than those of any other nation; but work harder, and must understand their duty well. Indeed if we had not had a good crew, our ship, being old, might have suffered severely.

In selecting this ship, in addition to accommodations, I only took into account her build; and so far was not disappointed, for when she *could* carry sail, she scudded along in gallant style; but with ships as with horses, the more they *have done*, the less they have *to do*.

I had a strong impression on my mind that a person travelling in America as a professed tourist, would be unable to form a correct estimate of the real character and condition of the people; for, from their great nationality, they would be likely to show him the best side of every thing. Of this kind of ostentation I very soon had a slight proof. Our ship left port in gallant trim, but had no sooner gained the open sea, than all hands were employed in stowing away the finery, and covering the rigging with mats—even the very cabin doors were taken off the hinges, and brass knobs and other ornaments which appeared to have been fixtures, were unshipped and deposited below, where they remained until our approach to New York, when the finery was again displayed, and all was placed once more *in statu quo*.

For the first twelve days we had rather pleasant weather, and nothing remarkable occurred, unless a swallow coming on board completely exhausted with flying, fatigue made it so tame that it suffered itself to be caressed; it however popped into the coop, and the ducks literally gobbled it up alive. The ducks were, same day, suffered to roam about the decks, and the pigs fell foul of one of them, and eat the breast off it. Passing the cabouse, I heard the negro steward soliloquising, and on looking in, perceived him cutting a hen's throat with the most heartfelt satisfaction, as he grinned and exclaimed, by way of answer to its screams, "Poor feller! I guess I wouldn't hurt you for de world;" I could not help thinking with Leibnitz, that most sapient of philosophers, that this is the best of all possible worlds.

On the thirteenth day we encountered a heavy gale, which continued to increase for four successive days. During this period we were unable to carry more canvass than was barely necessary to render the vessel manageable. A heavy gale, for the first time, is rather interesting than otherwise: the novelty of the sea's appearance—the anxiety of the crew and officers—the promptitude with which commands are given and executed—and the excitement produced by the other incidental occurrences, tend to make even a storm, when encountered in open sea, by no means destitute of pleasing interest. During this gale, the sailors appeared to be more than ordinarily anxious only upon one occasion, and then only for a minute—the circumstance was not calculated to create alarm in the mind of a person totally ignorant of nautical affairs, but being somewhat of a sailor, I understood the danger tolerably well. The helm was struck by a sea, and strained at the bolts; from the concussion occasioned by the blow, it was apprehended for a moment that it had been carried away. Without a helm, in such weather, much was to be feared; for her timbers being old, she could hardly meet the shock of an ocean wave upon her broadside without suffering serious injury. The helmsman was knocked down—the captain and mate jumped aft, to ascertain the extent of the damage; while the sailors scowled along the deck, as they laid their shoulders to the weather side of the ship—all was anxiety for the instant. At length the mate cried, "helm all right," and the crew pulled away as usual. At the close of the fourth day the storm subsided, and we approached the banks of Newfoundland.

It is generally supposed that the colour of the sea is a sure indication of the presence or absence of soundings; that is, that there are soundings where the water is green, and that there are none where the water is blue. The former is, I believe, true in every instance; but the latter is certainly not so, as the first soundings we got here, were in water as blue as indigo, depth fifty odd fathoms.

We were thirty days crossing these tiresome banks; during which time we were befogged, and becalmed, and annoyed with all sorts of disagreeable weather. The fogs or mists were frequently so dense, that it was impossible to see more than thirty yards from the vessel. This course is not that usually taken by ships bound for the United States, as they generally cross the Atlantic at much lower latitudes, but our captain "calculated" on escaping calms, and avoiding the influence of the Gulf stream, and thus making a quicker passage; he was, however, mistaken, as a packet ship that left Liverpool four days after, arrived at New York sixteen days before us.

We found the thermometer of incalculable service, both for ascertaining when we got into the stream, and for disclosing our dangerous proximity to icebergs. That we had approached near icebergs we discovered one evening to be the case by the mercury falling, suddenly, below 40°, in foggy weather. We notwithstanding held on our course, and fortunately escaped accident. Many vessels which depart from port with gallant crews, and are never heard of more, are lost, I am convinced, by fatal collision with these floating islands. From the beginning of spring to the latter end of summer, masses of brash ice are occasionally encountered in these latitudes.

Towards the evening of the fiftieth day we entered the bay of New York: the bay is really beautiful, and at this season (summer) perhaps appeared to the greatest advantage. The numerous islands with which it is interspersed, were covered to the water's edge with foliage and verdure, and here and there studded with handsome villas. The city appeared to be literally surrounded by a thick grove of masts, from which floated the flags of many nations—the scene, thus gradually unfolding itself to the eyes of one who had been for so long a time immured within a vessel, was really fascinating.

While at New York, I staid at the "Pearl-street Boarding-house," and experienced from Messrs. Haskell and Perry, the proprietors, the most polite attention. Most Europeans are astonished at the rapidity with which the Americans despatch their meals; but I, having admitted the proposition, that there was "nothing new under the sun," had long previously ceased to be *astonished* at any thing. On the first day of my dining at the table d'hôte, one of those gentlemen told me, when we sat down to dinner, that most of the persons at table were men of business, who were in the habit of eating much quicker than he knew I was accustomed to, and requested that that might not in the slightest interfere with my habits, but that I should entirely suit my own comfort and convenience. After that preface, I think I should have been most unreasonable to fall into a passion with the New Yorkers, because they *bolted* instead of masticating.

New York is altogether a trading place, and different from any thing of the same magnitude in Europe: scarcely a single street is exclusively filled with private residences;—in a mercantile point of view, it is the Liverpool of the United States.

The negros and mulattos constitute a considerable portion of the population. It is impossible to imagine the extreme ugliness of some of the sooty gentry; a decent ourang-outang might, without presumption, vie with many of these people, even of the *fair sex*, and an impartial judge should certainly decide that the said ourang-outang was the handsomer animal. Many of them are wealthy, and dress remarkably well. The females, when their shins and misshapen feet are concealed by long gowns, appear to have good figures. A few days after my arrival, walking down "Broadway" (the principal street) I was struck with the figure of a fashionably dressed woman, who was sauntering before me. After passing, I turned round, when—O angels and ministers of ugliness!—I beheld a face, as black as soot—a mouth that reached from ear to ear—a nose, like nothing human—and lips a full inch in diameter! On the following morning, whilst dressing at my bed-room window, I heard a squeaking sort of voice warbling forth, "Love was once a little Boy," and "I'd be a Butterfly." The strange *melody* and unusual intonations induced me to look out, when, to my astonishment, I found that the *fair* songstress was a most hideous-looking negress! Such are the scenes that constantly present themselves here, and remind a European that he is in a new region.

The white ladies dress fashionably, generally *à la Françoise*; have straight figures, and with the help of a little cotton, judiciously disposed, and sometimes, the smallest possible portion of rouge, contrive to look rather interesting; in general, they are lamentably deficient in *tournure* and *en-bon-point*. The hands and feet of the greatest belle, are *pas mignon*, and would be termed plebeian by the Anglo-Normans—the aristocracy of England. Yet I have seen many girls extremely handsome indeed, having a delicate bloom and fair skin; but this does not endure long, as the variable nature of the climate—the sudden and violent transitions of temperature which occur on this continent, destroy, in a few years, the complexion of the finest woman. When she arrives at the age of thirty, her skin is shrivelled and discoloured; she is thin, and has all the indications of premature old age. The women of England retain their beauty at least ten years longer than those of America.

The inhabitants of that part of New York nearest the shipping, are extremely sallow and unhealthy looking, and many have a most cadaverous aspect. Malaria certainly exists here in some degree. A man will tell you that the city is perfectly healthy, whilst his own appearance most unquestionably indicates disease. I speak now of the quays and adjacent streets; and the cause is very apparent. The wharfs are faced with wood, and the retiring of the tide exposes a rotten vegetable substance to the action of an almost tropical sun, which, added to the filth that is invariably found in the neighbourhood of shipping, is quite sufficient to produce the degree of unhealthiness that exists. On going up the town, the appearance of the inhabitants gradually improves, and approaching the suburbs, the difference is striking,—in this district I have seen persons as stout and healthy looking as any in England orIreland.

On the night of my arrival, a fire broke out, by which several extensive warehouses were entirely consumed. There is nothing more remarkable here than the frequent occurrence of this calamity, except the excellent arrangements that are made for arresting its progress. The engines, apparatus, and *corps de pompiers*, are admirably maintained, and the promptitude and regularity with which they arrive at the scene of devastation truly astonishing: indeed, were this not the case, the city must very soon be destroyed; for notwithstanding all their exertions, every conflagration makes it minus several houses, and few nights pass without bringing a misfortune of this nature.

There are several theatres, churches, and other public buildings, dispersed throughout the city. The City Hall, which stands near the upper end of a small enclosure, called the Park, is considered the handsomest building in the United States. It was finished in 1812, and cost half a million dollars.

The police regulations appear not to be so severe as they ought to be, for droves of hogs are permitted to roam about the streets, to the terror of fine ladies, and the great annoyance of all pedestrians.

New York was settled by the Dutch in 1615, and called by them New Amsterdam. In 1634, it was conquered by the English,—retaken by the Dutch in 1673, and restored in 1674. Its present population is estimated at 213,000.

Having heard that the celebrated Frances Wright, authoress of "A Few Days in Athens," was publicly preaching and promulgating her doctrines in the city, I determined on paying the "Hall of Science" a visit, in which establishment she usually lectured. The address she delivered on the evening I attended had been previously delivered on the fourth of July, in the city of Philadelphia; but, at the request of a numerous party of "Epicureans," she was induced to repeat it. The hall might contain perhaps ten or twelve hundred persons, and on this occasion it was filled to excess, by a well-dressed audience of both sexes.

The person of Frances Wright is tall and commanding—her features are rather masculine, and the melancholy cast which her countenance ordinarily assumes gives it rather a harsh appearance—her dark chestnut hair hangs in long graceful curls about her neck; and when delivering her lectures, her appearance is romantic and unique.

She is a speaker of great eloquence and ability, both as to the matter of her orations, and the manner of their delivery. The first sentence she utters rivets your attention; and, almost unconsciously, your sympathies are excited, and you are carried onward by the reasonings and the eloquence of this disciple of the Gardens. The impression made on the audience assembled on that occasion was really wonderful. Once or twice, when I could withdraw my attention from the speaker, I regarded the countenances of those around me, and certainly never witnessed any thing more striking. The high-wrought interest depicted in their faces, added to the breathless silence that reigned throughout the building, made the spectacle the most imposing I ever beheld. She was the Cumæan Sibyl delivering oracles and labouring under the inspiration of the God of Day.—This address was chiefly of a political character, and she took care to flatter the prejudices of the Americans, by occasionally recurring to the advantages their country possessed over European states—namely, the absence of country gentlemen, and of a church establishment; for to the absence of these the Americans attribute a large portion of the very great degree of comfort they enjoy.

Near Hoboken, about three miles up North river, at the opposite side to New York, a match took place between a boat rowed by two watermen, and a canoe paddled by two Indians. The boat was long and narrow, similar in form to those that ply on the Thames. The canoe was of the lightest possible construction, being composed of thin hickory ribs covered with bark. In calm weather, the Indians propel these vessels through the water with astonishing velocity; but when the wind is high, and the water much disturbed, their progress is greatly impeded. It so happened on this day that the water was rough, and consequently unfavourable to the Aborigines. At the appointed signal the competitors started. For a short distance the Indians kept up with their rivals, but the long heavy pull of the oar soon enabled the boatmen to leave them at a distance. The Indians, true to their character, seeing the contest hopeless, after the first turn, no longer contended for victory; they paddled deliberately back to the starting place, stepped out, and carried their canoe on shore. The superiority of the oar over the paddle was in this contest fully demonstrated.

CHAPTER II

Having determined on quitting "the London of the States," as my friends the Yankees call New York, I had bag and baggage conveyed on board a steamer bound for Albany. The arrangements and accommodations on board this boat were superb, and surpassed any thing of the kind I ever met with in Europe, on the same scale; and the groups of well-dressed passengers fully indicated the general prosperity of the country.

The distance between New York and Albany is about 165 miles. The scenery on the Hudson is said to be the most beautiful of any in America, and I believe cannot be surpassed in any country. Many of the beauties of rich European scenery are to be found along the banks of that noble river. In the highlands, about fifty miles from New York, is West Point, on which stands a strong fortress, containing an arsenal, a military-school, and a garrison. It is romantically situated among lofty crags and mountains, which rise above the level of the water from 1100 to 1500 feet. There are many handsome country seats and villages between West Point and Hudson, where the river is more than a mile wide.

After a passage of about sixteen or seventeen hours, we arrived at Albany. The charge for passage, including dinner and tea, was only three dollars; and the day following the cost was reduced, through the spirit of opposition, to one dollar.

Albany is the legislative capital of New York. It is a handsome city, and one of the oldest in the Union. Most of the houses are built of wood, which, when tastefully painted (not often the case) have rather a pleasing appearance. The situation of this city is advantageous, both from the direct communication which it enjoys with the Atlantic, by means of sloops and schooners, and the large tract of back country which it commands. A trade with Canada is established by means of the Erie and Hudson canal. The capitol, and other public buildings, are large and handsome, and being constructed of either brick or stone, give the city a respectable appearance.

Albany, in 1614, was first settled by the Dutch, and was by them called Orange. On its passing into the hands of the English, in 1664, its present name was given to it, in honour of the Duke of York. It was chartered in 1686.

From Albany I proceeded along the canal, by West Troy and Junction, and near the latter place we came to Cohoe's Falls, on the Mohawk. The river here is about 250 yards wide, which rushing over a jagged and uneven bed of rocks, produces a very picturesque effect. The canal runs nearly parallel with this river from Junction to Utica, crossing it twice, at an interval of seven miles, over aqueducts nearly fifty rods in length, constructed of solid beams of timber. The country is very beautiful, and for the most part well cultivated. The soil possesses every variety of good and bad. The farms along the canal are valuable, land being generally worth from fifty to a hundred dollars per acre.

Above Schenectady, a very ancient town, the bed of the canal gave way, which of course obliged us to come to a dead halt. I hired, for myself and two others, a family waggon (dignified here with the appellation of *carriage*) to take us beyond the break, in expectation of being able to get a boat thence onwards, but unfortunately all the upward-bound boats had proceeded. We were, therefore, obliged to wait until next morning. My fellow travellers having light luggage, got themselves and it into a hut at the other side of the lock; but I, having heavy baggage, which it was impossible to carry across, was compelled to remain on the banks, between the canal and the Mohawk, all night. On the river there were several canoes, with fishermen spearing by torch-light; while on the banks the boatmen and boys, Mulattos and whites, were occupied in gambling. They had tables, candles, dice, and cards. With these, and with a *quantum sufficit* of spirits, they contrived to while away the time until day-break; of course interlarding their conversation with a reasonable quantity of oaths and imprecations. The breach being repaired early in the morning, the boats came up, and we proceeded to Utica.

Seven miles above Utica is seated Rome, a small and dirty town, bearing no possible resemblance to the "Eternal City," even in its more modern condition, as the residence of the "Triple Prince;" but, on the contrary, having, if one could judge from the habitations, every appearance of squalid poverty. Fifteen miles further on, we passed the Little Falls. It was night when we came to them, but it being moonlight, we had an opportunity of seeing them to advantage. The crags are here stupendous—irregular and massive piles of rocks, from which spring the lofty pine and cedar, are heaped in frightful disorder on each other, and give the scene a terrifically grand appearance.

From Rome to Syracuse, a distance of forty-six miles, the canal is cut through a swampy forest, a great portion of which is composed of dead trees. One of the most dismal scenes imaginable is a forest of charred trees, which is occasionally to be met with in this country, especially in the route by which I was travelling. It is caused by the woods being fired, by accident or otherwise. The aspect of these blasted monuments of ruined vegetation is strange and peculiar; and the air of desertion and desolation which pervades their neighbourhood, reminds one of the stories that are told of the Upas valley of Java, for here too not a bird is to be seen. The smell arising from this swamp in the night, was so bad as to oblige us to shut all the windows and doors of the boat, which, added to the bellowing and croaking of the bull frogs—the harsh and incessant noise of the grasshoppers, and the melancholy cry of the whip-poor-will, formed a combination not of the most agreeable nature. Yet, in defiance of all this, we were induced occasionally to brave the terrors of the night, in order to admire that beautiful insect the fire-fly, or as it is called by the natives, "lightning bug." They emit a greenish phosphorescent light, and are seen at this season in every part of the country. The woods here were full of them, and seemed literally to be studded with small stars, which emitted a bright flickering light.

After you pass Syracuse, the country begins to improve; but still it is low and marshy, and for the most part unhealthy, as the appearance of the people clearly indicates. In this country, as in every other, the canals are generally cut through comparatively low lands, and the low lands here, with few exceptions, are all swampy; however, a great deal of the unhealthiness which pervades this district, arises from want of attention. A large portion of the inhabitants are Low Dutch, who appear never to be in their proper element, unless when settled down in the midst of a swamp. They allow rotten timber to accumulate, and stagnant pools to remain about their houses, and from these there arises an effluvium which is most unpleasant in warm weather, which, however, they do not seem to perceive.

We entered Rochester, through an aqueduct thirty rods in length, built of stone, across the Genessee river. Rochester is the handsomest town on this line. Some of the houses here are tastefully decorated. All the windows have Venetian blinds, and generally there are one or two covered balconies attached to the front of each house. Before the doors there are small *parterres*, planted with rose-trees, and other fragrant shrubs. About half a mile from the town are the Falls of Genessee. The water glides over an even bed of limestone rock, ninety-six feet above the level of the river below. There is a beautiful regularity in this fall, but its extreme uniformity divests it of picturesque effect. Here the celebrated diver, Sam. Patch, subsequently met his fate in diving off this precipice. He had performed similar feats at the Falls of Niagara, without sustaining any injury. He was not killed by the fall; but is supposed to have fainted when midway from, his leap, as his arms were observed to relax, and his legs to open, before he reached the water.

On my journey I met with an Englishman, a Mr. W——. He dressed *à la Mungo Park*, wearing a jacket and trowsers of jean, and a straw hat. He was a great pedestrian; had travelled through most of the southern States, and was now on his tour through this part of the country. He was a gentleman about fifty,—silent and retiring in his habits. Enamoured of the orange-trees of Georgia, he intended returning there or to Carolina, and ending his days. We agreed to visit the Falls of Niagara together, and accordingly quitted the boat at Tonawanta. When we had dined, and had deposited our luggage in the safe keeping of the Niagara hotel-keeper, my companion shouldered his vigne stick, and to one end of which he appended a small bundle, containing a change of linen, &c., and I put on my shooting coat of many pockets, and shouldered my gun. Thus equipped, we commenced our journey to the Great Falls. The distance from Tonawanta to the village of the Falls, now called Manchester, is about eleven miles. The way lies through a forest, in which there are but a few scattered habitations. A great part of the road runs close to the river Niagara; and the occasional glimpses of this broad sheet of water, which are obtained through the rich foliage of the forest, added to the refreshing breeze that approached us through the openings, rendered our pedestrian excursion extremely delightful.

Towards evening we arrived at the village, and proceeded to reconnoitre, in order to fix our position for the night. After having done this satisfactorily, we then turned our attention to the all-important operation of eating and drinking. While supping, an eccentric-looking person passed out through the apartment in which we were. His odd appearance excited our curiosity, and we inquired who this mysterious-looking gentleman was. We were informed that he was an Englishman, and that he had been lodging there for the last six months, but that he concealed his real name. He slept in one corner of a large barrack room, in which there were of course several other beds. On a small table by his bed-side there were a few French and Latin books, and some scraps of poetry touching on the tender passion. These, and a German flute, which we observed standing against the window, gave us some clue to his character. He was a tall, romantic-looking young man, apparently about twenty-seven or twenty-eight years of age. His dress was particularly shabby. This the landlord told us was from choice, not from necessity, as he had two trunks full of clothes nearly new. The reason he gave for dressing as he did, was his knowing, he said, that if he dressed well, people would be talking to him, which he wished to avoid; but, that by dressing as he did, he made sure that no one would ever think of giving him any annoyance of that kind. I thought this idea unique: and whether he be still at Niagara, or has taken up his abode at the foot of the Rocky mountains, I pronounce him to be a Diogenes without a tub. He has read at least one page in the natural history of civilized man.

We visited the Falls, at the American side by moonlight. There was then an air of grandeur and sublimity in the scene which I shall long remember. Yet at this side they are not seen to the greatest advantage. Next morning I crossed the Niagara river, below the Falls, into Canada. I did not ascend the bank to take the usual route to the Niagara hotel, at which place there is a spiral staircase descending 120 feet towards the foot of the Falls, but clambered along at the base of the cliffs until I reached the point immediately below the stairs. I here rested, and indeed required it much, for the day was excessively warm, and I had unfortunately encumbered myself with my gun and shot pouch. The Falls are here seen in all their grandeur. Two immense volumes of water glide over perpendicular precipices upwards of 170 feet in height, and tumble among the crags below with a roaring that *we* distinctly heard on our approach to the village, at the distance of five miles up the river: and down the river it can be heard at a much greater distance. The Falls are divided by Goat Island into two parts. The body of water which falls to the right of the island is much greater than that which falls to the left; and the cliffs to the right assume the form of a horse-shoe. To the left there is also a considerable indentation, caused by a late falling in of the rock; but it scarcely appears from the Canadian side. The rushing of the waters over such immense precipices—the dashing of the spray, which rises in a white cloud at the base of the Falls, and is felt at the distance of a quarter of a mile—the many and beautiful rainbows that occasionally appear,—united, form a grand and imposing *coup d'oeil.*

The Fall is supposed to have been originally at the table-land near Lewiston; and indeed, from the nature of the ground, and its present condition below the Falls, no reasonable objection can be entertained to that supposition. The upper part of the cliffs is composed of hard limestone, and underneath is a bed of schistus. Now this schistus is continually worn away by the water's dashing against it. This leaves the upper part, or immediate bed of the river, without foundation. When, therefore, from extraordinary floods, the pressure of the incumbent fluid becomes more than usually great, the rock gives way; and thus, gradually, the Falls have receded several miles.

I at length ascended the stairs, and popped my head into the shanty, *sans ceremonie*, to the no small amazement of the cunning compounder of "cock-tails," and "mint julaps" who presided at the bar. It was clear that I had ascended the stairs, but how the deuce I had got down was the question. I drank my "brandy sling," and retreated before he had recovered from his surprise, and thus I escaped the volley of interrogatories with which I should have been most unsparingly assailed. I walked for some distance along the Canadian heights, and then crossed the river, where I met my friend waiting my return under a clump of scrub oak.

We had previously determined on visiting the Tuscarora village, an Indian settlement about eight miles down the river, and not far from Ontario. This is a tribe of one of the six nations, the last that was admitted into the Confederation. They live in a state of community; and in their arrangements for the production and distribution of wealth, approach nearer to the Utopean system than any community with which I am acquainted. The squaws told us that no Indian there could claim any thing but what was contained within his own cabin; that the produce of the land was common property, and that they never quarrelled about its division. We dined in one of their cabins, on lean mutton and corn bread. The interior of their habitations is not conspicuous for cleanliness; nor are they so far civilized as to be capable of breaking their word. The people at the Niagara village told us, that with the exception of two individuals in that community, any Indian could get from them on credit either money or goods to whatever amount he required.

I here parted with my fellow traveller, perhaps for ever. He went to Lewiston, whence he intended to cross into Canada, and to walk along the shores of Ontario; whilst I made the best of my way back through the woods to Manchester. I certainly think our landlord had some misgivings respecting the fate of my companion. We had both departed together: I alone was armed—and I alone returned. However, as I unflinchingly stood examination and cross-examination, and sojourned until next morning, his fears seemed to be entirely dispelled. Next day I took a long, last look at Niagara, and departed for Tonawanta.

At Tonawanta I again took the canal-boat to Buffalo, a considerable town on the shores of lake Erie, and at the head of the canal navigation. There are several good buildings in this town, and some well-appointed hotels. Lake schooners, and steam and canal boats are here in abundance, it being an entrepôt for western produce and eastern merchandize. A few straggling Indians are to be seen skulking about Buffalo, like dogs in Cairo, the victims of the inordinate use of ardent spirits.

From Buffalo I proceeded in a steamer along lake Erie, to Portland in Ohio, now called Sandusky City; the distance 240 miles. After about an hour's sail, we entirely lost sight of the Canadian shores. The scenery on the American side is very fine, particularly from Presqu' Isle onward to the head of the lake, or rather from its magnitude, it might be termed an inland sea.

On landing at Sandusky, I learned that there were several Indian reserves between that place and Columbus, the seat of government. This determined me on making a pedestrian tour to that city. Accordingly, having forwarded my luggage, and made other necessary arrangements, I commenced my pergrinations among the Aborigines.

The woods in the upper part of Ohio, nearest the lake, are tolerably open, and occasionally interspersed with sumach and sassafras: the soil somewhat sandy. I met with but few Indians, until my arrival at Lower Sandusky, on the Sandusky river; here there were several groups returning to their reserves, from Canada, where they had been to receive the annual presents made them by the British government. In the next county (Seneca) there is a reservation of about three miles square, occupied by Senecas, Cayugas, and part of the Iroquois or six nations, once a most powerful confederation amongst the red men.[1] In Crawford county there is a very large reserve belonging to the Huron or Wyandot Indians. These, though speaking a dialect of the Iroquois tongue, are more in connexion with the Delawares than with the Iroquois. The Wyandots are much esteemed by their white neighbours, for probity and good behaviour. They dress very tastefully. A handsome chintz shawl tied in the Moorish fashion about the head—leggings of blue cloth, reaching half way up the thigh, sewn at the outside, leaving a hem of about an inch deep—mocassins, or Indian boots, made of deer-skin, to fit the foot close, like a glove—a shirt or tunic of white calico—and a hunting shirt, or frock, made of strong blue-figured cotton or woollen cloth, with a small fringed cape, and long sleeves,—a tomahawk and scalping knife stuck in a broad leather belt. Accoutred in this manner, and mounted on a small hardy horse, called here an Indian pony, imagine a tall, athletic, brown man, with black hair and eyes—the hair generally plaited in front, and sometimes hanging in long wavy curls behind—aquiline nose, and fearless aspect, and you have a fair idea of the Wyandot and Cayuga Indian. The Senecas and Oneidas whom I met with, were not so handsome in general, but as athletic, and about the same average height—five feet nine or ten.

The Indians here, as every where else, are governed by their own laws, and never have recourse to the whites to settle their disputes. That silent unbending spirit, which has always characterized the Indian, has alone kept in check the rapacious disposition of the whites. Several attempts have been made to induce the Indians to sell their lands, and go beyond the Mississippi, but hitherto without effect. The Indian replies to the fine speeches and wily language of the whites, "We hold this small bit of land, in the vast country of our fathers, by *your* written talk, and it is noted on *our* wampums—the bones of our fathers lie here, and we cannot forsake them. You tell us our great father (the president) is powerful, and that his arm is long and strong—we believe it is so; but we are in hopes that he will not strike his red children for their lands, and that he will leave us this little piece to live upon—the hatchet is long buried, let it not be disturbed."

Jackson has lately published a manifesto to all the Indian tribes within the limits of the United States, commanding them to sell their reserves; and with few exceptions, has been answered in this manner.

A circumstance occurred a few days previous to my arrival, in the Seneca reserve, which may serve to illustrate the determined character of the Indian. There were three brothers (chiefs) dwelling in this reservation. "Seneca John," the eldest brother, was the principal chief of the tribe, and a man much esteemed by the white people. He died by poison. The chiefs in council, having satisfactorily ascertained that his second brother "Red-hand," and a squaw, had poisoned him, decreed that Red-hand should be put to death. "Black-snake," the other brother, told the chiefs that if Red-hand must die, he himself would kill him, in order to prevent feuds arising in the tribe. Accordingly in the evening he repaired to the hut of Red-hand, and after having sat in silence for some time, said, "My best chiefs say, you have killed my father's son,—they say my brother must die." Red-hand merely replied, "They say so;" and continued to smoke. After about fifteen minutes further silence, Black-snake said, pointing to the setting sun, "When he appears above those trees"—moving his arm round to the opposite direction—"I come to kill you." Red-hand nodded his head in the short significant style of the Indian, and said "Good." The next morning Black-snake came, followed by two chiefs, and having entered the hut, first put out the squaw, he then returned and stood before his brother, his eyes bent on the ground. Red-hand said calmly, "Has my brother come that I may die?"—"It is so," was the reply. "Then," exclaimed Red-hand, grasping his brother's left hand with his own right, and dashing the shawl from his head, "Strike sure!" In an instant the tomahawk was from the girdle of Black-snake, and buried in the skull of the unfortunate man. He received several blows before he fell, uttering the exclamation "hugh," each time. The Indians placed him on the grass to die, where the backwoodsman who told me the story, saw him after the lapse of two hours, and life was not then extinct,—with such tenacity does it cling to the body of an Indian. The scalping knife was at length passed across his throat, and thus ended the scene.

From Sandusky city, in Huron county, I passed into Sandusky county, and from thence through Seneca county. These three counties are entirely woodlands, with the exception of a few small prairies which lay eastward of my course. The land is generally fertile. Some light sandy soil is occasionally to be met with, which produces more quickly than the heavier soil, but not so abundantly. I saw in my travels through these counties a few persons who were ill of ague-fever, as it is here called. The prevalence of this disease is not to be attributed to a general unhealthiness of the climate, but can at all times be referred to localities.

I next entered Crawford county, and crossed the Wyandot prairie, about seven miles in length, to Upper Sandusky. This was the first of those extensive meadows I had seen, and I was much pleased with its appearance—although this prairie is comparatively but small, yet its beauty cannot be surpassed; and the groves, and clusters of trees, *iles de bois*, with which it is interspersed, make it much resemble a beautiful domain.

Attached to the Wyandot reserve (nine miles by sixteen) is that of the Delawares (three miles square). On reaching Little Sandusky—Kahama's curse on the town baptizers of America!—there are often five or six places named alike in one state: upper and lower, little and big, great and small—and invariably the same names that are given to towns in one State, are to be found in every other. Then their vile plagiarisms of European names causes a Babelonish confusion of ideas, enough to disturb the equanimity of a "grisly saint;" and, with all humility, I disclaim having any pretensions to that character. I have frequently heard a long-legged, sallow-looking backwoodsman talk of having come lately from Paris, or Mecca, when instead of meaning the capital of *La grande nation*, or the city of "the holy prophet," he spoke of some town containing a few hundred inhabitants, situated in the backwoods of Kentucky, or amidst the gloomy forests of Indiana. The Americans too speak in prospective, when they talk of great places; no doubt "calculating" that, one day, all the mighty productions of the old world will be surpassed by their ingenuity and perseverance.

I reached Little Sandusky about one o'clock in the day, and there learned that there was a treaty being holden with the Delawares—accordingly I repaired to the council ground. On a mat, under the shade of seven large elm trees, which in more prosperous times had waved over the war-like ancestors of this unfortunate people, were seated three old sachems, the principal of the tribe. The oldest appeared to be nearly eighty years of age, the next about seventy, and the last about fifty. On a chair to the right of the Indians was seated a young "half-breed" chief, the son of one of the sachems by a white squaw; and on their left, seated on another chair, a Delaware dressed in the costume of the whites. This young man was in the pay of the States, and acted as interpreter—he interpreting into and from the Delaware language, and a gentleman of the mission (a Captain Walker) into and from the Wyandot. At a table opposite the Indians were seated the commissioners.

The Lenni Lenapé, or Delawares, as they were called by the English, from the circumstance of their holding their great "Council-fire" on the banks of the Delaware river, were once the most powerful of the several tribes that spoke the Delaware tongue, and possessed an immense tract of country east of the Alleghany mountains. This unfortunate people had been driven from place to place, until at last they were obliged to accept of an asylum from the Wyandot, whom they call their uncle; and now are forced to sell this, and go beyond the Mississippi. To a reflecting mind, the scene was touching beyond description. Here was the sad remnant of a great nation, who having been forced back from the original country of their fathers, by successive acts of rapacity, are now compelled to enter into a compact which obliges them, half civilized as they are, to return to the forest. The case is this,—the white people, or rather Jackson and the southerns, say, that the Indians "retard improvement"—precisely in the same sense that a brigand, when he robs a traveller, might say, that the traveller retarded improvement—that is, retarded *his* improvement, inasmuch as he had in his pocket, what would improve the condition of the brigand. The Indians have cultivated farms, and valuable tracts of land, and no doubt it will improve the condition of the whites, to get possession of those farms and rich lands, for *one tenth of their saleable value.* The profits that have accrued to the United States from the systematic plunder of the Indians, are immense, and a great portion of the national debt has been liquidated by this dishonest means.[2]

The reserve of the Delawares contained nine square miles, or 5760 acres. For this it was agreed at the treaty, that they should be paid 6000 dollars, and the value of the improvements, which I conceived to be a fair bargain. I was not then aware of the practice pursued by the government, of making deductions, under various pretences, from the purchase-money, until the unfortunate Indian is left scarcely anything in lieu of his lands, and says, that "the justice of the white man is not like the justice of the red man," and that he cannot understand the honesty of his Christian brother. The following extract, taken from the New York American, will give some insight into the mode of dealing with the Indians.

"*The last of the Ottowas.*—Maumee Bay, Ohio, Sept. 3, 1831.—Mr. James B. Gardiner has concluded a very important treaty at Maumee Bay, in Michigan, for a cession of all the lands owned by the Ottowa Indians in Ohio, about 50,000 acres. It was attended with more labour and greater difficulties than any other treaty made in this state: it was the last foothold which that savage, warlike, and hostile tribe held in their ancient dominion. The conditions of this treaty are very similar to those treaties of Lewistown and Wapaghkenetta, *with this exception*, that the surplus avails of their lands, *after deducting seventy cents per acre to indemnify the government*, are to be appropriated for paying the debts of their nation, which amount to about 20,000 dollars." [Query, what are those debts?—could they be the amount of *presents* made them on former occasions?] "The balance, *if any*, accrues to the tribe. Seventy thousand acres of land are granted to them west of the Mississippi.[3] The Ottowas are the most depredating, drunken, and ferocious in Ohio. The reservations ceded by them are very valuable, and those on the Miami of the lake embrace some of the best mill privileges in the State."

The Delawares were too few (being but fifty-one in number) to contend the matter, and therefore accepted of the proposed terms. At the conclusion of the conference, the Commissioners told them that they should have a barrel of flour, with the beef that had been killed for the occasion, which was received with "Yo-ha!—Yo-ha!" They then said, laughing, "that they hoped their father would allow them a little milk," meaning whisky, which was accordingly granted. They drank of this modern Lethé and forgot for a time their misfortunes.

On the Osage fork of the Merrimack river, there are two settlements of the Delawares, to the neighbourhood of which these Indians intend to remove.

Near the Delaware reserve, I fell in with a young Indian, apparently about twenty years of age, and we journeyed together for several miles through the forest. He spoke English fluently, and conformed as far as his taste would permit him, to the habits of the whites. His dress consisted of a blue frock coat, blue cloth leggings, moccasins, a shawl tied about the head, and a red sash round his waste. In conversation, I asked him if he were not a Cayuga—: "No," says he, "an Oneida," placing both his hands on his breast—"a *clear* Oneida." I could not help smiling at his national pride;—yet this is man: in every country and condition he is proud of his descent, and loves the race to which he belongs. This Oneida was a widow's son. He had sixteen acres of cleared land, which, with occasional assistance, he cultivated himself. When the produce was sold, he divided the proceeds with his mother, and then set out, and travelled until his funds were exhausted. He had just then returned from a tour to New York and Philadelphia, and had visited almost every city in the Union. As Guedeldk—that was the Oneida's name—and I were rambling along, we met a negro who was journeying in great haste—he stopped to inquire if we had seen that day, or the day previous, any nigger-woman going towards the lake. I had passed the day before two waggon loads of negros, which were being transported, by the state, to Canada. A local law prohibits the settlement of people of colour within the state of Ohio, which was now put in force, although it had remained dormant for many years.

There was much hardship in the case of this poor fellow. He had left his family at Cincinnati, and had gone to work on the canal some eighteen or twenty miles distant. He had been absent about a week; and on his return he found his house empty, and was informed that his wife and children had been seized, and transported to Canada. The enforcement of this law has been since abandoned; and I must say, although the law itself is at variance with the Constitution of the United States, which is paramount to all other laws, that its abandonment is due entirely to the good feeling of the people of Ohio, who exclaimed loudly against the cruelty of the measure.

FOOTNOTES:

[1]

De Witt Clinton, speaking of the Iroquois, or five nations, says, "Their exterior relations, general interests, and national affairs, were conducted and superintended by a great council, assembled annually in Onondaga, the central canton, composed of the chiefs of each republic; and eighty sachems were frequently convened at this national assembly. It took cognizance of the great questions of war and peace; of the affairs of the tributary nations, and their negotiations with the French and English colonies. All their proceedings were conducted with great deliberation, and were distinguished for order, decorum, and solemnity. In eloquence, in dignity, and in all the characteristics of profound policy, they surpassed the assembly of feudal barons, and perhaps were not inferior to the great Amphictyonic Council of Greece."

[2]

	Dollars.
Amount of lands sold up to the year 1824	44,229,837
173,176,606 acres unsold, estimated at one dollar per acre. The Congress price was then two dollars, but was subsequently reduced to a dollar and a quarter, and is now 75 cents.	173,176,606
	217,406,443
Deduct value of annuities, expenses of surveying, &c. &c., being the amount of purchase-money paid for same	4,243,632
Profit arising to the United States from purchases of land from the Indians	213,162,811

Allowing 480 cents, to the pound sterling, the gross profit is £44,408,918. 19*s*. 2*d*.

[3]

There are lands west of the Mississippi, which would be dear at ten cents per hundred acres.

CHAPTER III

From Little Sandusky, I passed through Marion, in Marion county. This town, like most others in Ohio, is advancing rapidly, and has at present several good brick buildings. The clap-boarded frame houses, which compose the great mass of habitations in the towns throughout the western country, in general have a neat appearance. I here saw gazetted three divorces, all of which had been granted on the applications of the wives. One, on the ground of the husband's absenting himself for one year: another, on account of a blow having been given: and the third for general neglect. There are few instances of a woman's being refused a divorce in the western country, as dislike is very generally—and very rationally—supposed to constitute a sufficient reason for granting the ladies their freedom.

I crossed Delaware county into Franklin county, where Columbus, the capital of the state, is situated. The roads from the lake to this city, with few exceptions, passed through woodlands, and the country is but thinly settled. Beech, oak, elm, hickory, walnut, white-oak, ash, &c. compose the bulk of the forest trees; and in the bottom lands, enormous sycamores are to be seen stretching their white arms almost to the very clouds. The land is of various denominations, but in general may be termed fertile.

Columbus, the capital of Ohio, is seated on the Scioto river, which is navigable for keel and flat boats, and small craft, almost to its source; and by means of a portage of about four miles, to Sandusky river, which flows into lake Erie, a convenient communication is established between the lakes, and the great western waters. The town is well laid out. The streets are wide; and the court-house, town-hall, and public offices, are built of brick. There are some good taverns here, and the tables d'hôtes are well and abundantly supplied.

There are land offices in every county seat, in which maps and plans of the county are kept. On these, the disposable tracts of country are distinguished from those which have been disposed of. The purchaser pays one fourth of the purchase money, for which he gets a receipt,—this constitutes his title, until, on paying the residue, he receives a regular title deed. He may however pay the full amount at once, and receive a discount of, I believe, eight per cent. A township comprises thirty-six square miles (twenty three thousand and forty acres) in sections of six hundred and forty acres each, which are subdivided, to accommodate purchasers, into quarter sections, or lots of a hundred and sixty acres. The sixteenth section is not sold, but reserved for the support of the poor, for education, and other public uses. There is no provision made in this, or any other state, for the ministers of religion, which is found to be highly beneficial to the interests of practical Christianity. The congress price of land has lately been reduced from a dollar and a quarter per acre, to seventy-five cents.

Ohio averages 184 miles in extent, from north to south, and 220 miles from east to west. Area, 40,000 square miles, or 25,600,000 acres. The population in 1790, was 3000; in 1800, 45,365; in 1810, 230,760; and in 1820, 581,434. White males, 300,609; white females, 275,955; free people of colour, 4723; militia in 1821, 83,247. The last census, taken in 1830, makes the population 937,679.

Having no more Indian reserves to visit, I took the stage, and rumbled over corduroys, republicans, stumps, and ruts, until my ribs were literally sore, through London, Xenia, and Lebanon, to Cincinnati.

At Lebanon there is a large community of the shaking Quakers. They have establishments also in Mason county, and at Covington, in Kentucky: their tenets are strictly Scriptural. They contend, that confessing their sins to one another, is necessary to a state of perfection; that the church of Christ ought to have all things in common; that none of the members of this church ought to cohabit, but be literally virgins; and that to dance and be merry is their duty, which part of their doctrines they take from the thirty-first chapter of Jeremiah.

Their ceremonies are as follows:—The men sit on the left hand, squatting on the floor, with their knees up, and their hands clasped round them. Opposite, in the same posture, sit the women, whose appearance is most cadaverous and sepulchral, dressed in the Quaker costume. After sitting for some time in this hatching position, they all rise and sing a canting sort of hymn, during which the women keep time by elevating themselves on their toes. After the singing has ceased, a discourse is delivered by one of the elders; which being ended, the men pull off their coats and waistcoats. All being prepared, one of the brethren steps forward to the centre of the room, and in a loud voice, gives out a tune, beating time with his foot, and singing *lal lal la, lal lal la*, &c., being joined by the whole group, all jumping as high as possible, clapping their hands, and at intervals twirling round,—but making rather ungraceful *pirouettes*: this exercise they continue until they are completely exhausted. In their ceremonials they much resemble the howling Dervishes of the Moslems, whom they far surpass in fanaticism.

Within about ten miles of Cincinnati we took up an old doctor, who was going to that city for the purpose of procuring a warrant against one of his neighbours, who, he had reason to believe, was concerned in the kidnapping of a free negro the night before. This is by no means an uncommon occurrence in the free states bordering the great rivers. The unfortunate black man, when captured, is hurried down to the river, thrust into a flat boat, and carried to the plantations. Such negros are not exposed for sale in the public bazaars, as that would be attended with risk; but a false bill of sale is made out, and the sale is effected to some planter before they reach Orleans. There is, of course, always collusion between the buyer and seller, and the man is disposed of, generally, for half his value.

These are certainly atrocious acts; yet when a British subject reads such passages as the following, in the histories of East India government, he must feel that if they were ten times as infamous and numerous as they are in reality, it becomes not *him* to censure them. Bolts, who was a judge of the mayor's court of Calcutta, says, in his "Considerations on India Affairs," page 194, "With every species of monopoly, therefore, every kind of oppression to manufacturers of all denominations throughout the whole country has daily increased; insomuch that weavers, for daring to sell their goods, and Dallals and Pykars, for having contributed to, or connived at, such sales, have by the *Company's agents,* been frequently seized and imprisoned, confined in irons, fined considerable sums of money, flogged, and deprived, in the most ignominious manner, of what they esteem most valuable, their castes. Weavers also, upon their inability to perform such agreements as have been *forced from them by the Company's agents*, universally known in Bengal by the name of *Mutchulcahs*, have had their goods seized and sold on the spot, to make good the deficiency: and the winders of raw silk, called *Nagaards,* have been treated also with such injustice, that instances have been known of their cutting off their thumbs, to prevent their being forced to wind silk. This last kind of workmen were pursued with such rigour, during Lord Clive's late government in Bengal, from a zeal for *increasing the Company's investment* of raw silk, that the most sacred laws of society were atrociously violated; for it was *a common thing for the Company's scapoys* to be sent by force of arms to break open the houses of the Armenian merchants established at Sydabad (who have from time immemorial been largely concerned in the silk trade), and forcibly take the *Nagaards* from their work, and carry them away to the English factory."

As we approached Cincinnati the number of farms, and the extent of cultivated country, indicated the comparative magnitude of that city. Fields in this country have nothing like the rich appearance of those in England and Ireland, being generally filled with half-rotten stumps, scattered here and there among the growing corn, producing a most disagreeable effect. Then, instead of the fragrant quickset hedge, there is a "worm fence"—the rudest description of barrier known in the country—which consists simply of bars, about eight or nine feet in length, laid zig-zag on each other alternately: the improvement on this, and the *ne plus ultra* in the idea of a west country farmer, is what is termed a "post and rail fence." This denomination of fence is to be seen sometimes in the vicinity of the larger towns, and is constructed of posts six feet in length, sunk in the ground to the depth of about a foot, and at eight or ten feet distance; the rails are then laid into mortises cut into the posts, at intervals of about thirteen or fourteen inches, which completes the work.

Cincinnati is built on a bend of the Ohio river, which takes here a semicircular form, and runs nearly west; it afterwards flows in a more southerly direction. A complete chain of hills, sweeping from one point of the bend round to the other, encloses the city in a sort of amphitheatre. The houses are mostly brick, and the streets all paved. There are several spacious and handsome market houses, which on market days are stocked with all kinds of provisions—indeed I think the market of Cincinnati is very nearly the best supplied in the United States. There are many respectable public buildings here, such as a court-house, theatre, bazaar, (built by Mrs. Trollope, but the speculation failed), and divers churches, in which you may see well-dressed women, and hear orthodox, heterodox, and every other species of doctrine, promulgated and enforced by strength of lungs, and length of argument, with pulpit-drum accompaniment, and all other requisites *ad captandum vulgus*.

The city stands on two plains: one called the bottom, extends about 260 yards back from the river, and is three miles in length, from Deer Creek to Mill Creek; the other is fifty feet higher than the first, and is called the Hill; this extends back about a mile. The bottom is sixty-five feet above low water mark. In 1815 the population was estimated at 6000, and at present it is supposed to be upwards of 25,000 souls. By means of the Dayton canal, which runs from that town nearly parallel with the "Big Miami" river, a very extensive trade, for all kinds of produce, is established with the back country. Steamers are constantly arriving at, and departing from the wharf, on their passage up and down the river. This is one of the many examples to be met with in the western country, of towns springing into importance within the memory of comparatively young men—a log-house is still standing, which is shewn as the first habitation built by the backwoodsman, who squatted in the forest where now stands a handsome and flourishing city.

On arriving at Cincinnati, I learned that my friend T—— had taken up his abode at a farm-house a few miles from town, where I accordingly repaired, and found him in good health, and initiated into all the manners, habits, customs, and diversions of the natives. Farming people in Ohio work hard.

The women have no sinecures, being occupied the greater part of the day in cooking; as they breakfast at eight, dine at half-past twelve, and sup at six, and at each of these meals, meat, and other cooked dishes are served up. In farming they co-operate with each other. When a farmer wishes to have his corn husked, he rides round to his neighbours and informs them of his intention. An invitation of this kind was once given in my presence. The farmer entered the house, sat down, and after the customary compliments were passed, in the usual laconic style, the following dialogue took place. "I guess I'll husk my corn to-morrow afternoon."—"You've a mighty heap this year."—"Considerable of corn." The host at length said, "Well, I guess we'll be along"—and the matter was arranged. All these gatherings are under the denomination of "frolics"—such as "corn-husking frolic," "apple-cutting frolic," "quilting frolic," &c.

Being somewhat curious in respect to national amusements, I attended a "corn-husking frolic" in the neighbourhood of Cincinnati. The corn was heaped up into a sort of hillock close by the granary, on which the young "Ohiohians" and "buck-eyes"—the lasses of Ohio are called "buck-eyes"—seated themselves in pairs; while the old wives, and old farmers were posted around, doing little, but talking much. Now the laws of "corn-husking frolics" ordain, that for each red ear that a youth finds, he is entitled to exact a kiss from his partner. There were two or three young Irishmen in the group, and I could observe the rogues kissing half-a-dozen times on the same red ears. Each of them laid a red-ear close by him, and after every two or three he'd husk, up he'd hold the redoubtable red-ear to the astonished eyes of the giggling lass who sate beside him, and most unrelentingly inflict the penalty. The "gude wives" marvelled much at the unprecedented number of red-ears which that lot of corn contained: by-and-by, they thought it "a kind of curious" that the Irishmen should find so many of them—at length, the cheat was discovered, amidst roars of laughter. The old farmers said the lads were "wide awake," and the "buck-eyes" declared that there was no being up to the plaguy Irishmen "no how," for they were always sure to have every thing their own way. But the mischief of it was, the young Americans took the hint, and the poor "buck-eyes" got nothing like fair play for the remainder of that evening. All agreed that there was more laughing, and more kissing done at that, than had been known at any corn-husking frolic since "the Declaration."

The farmers of Ohio are a class of people about equivalent to our second and third rate farmer, inasmuch as they work themselves, but possessing infinitely more independence in their character and deportment. Every white male, who is a citizen of the United States, and has resided one year in the state, and paid taxes, has a vote. The members of the legislature are elected annually, and those of the senate biennially; half of the members of the latter branch vacating their seats every year. The representatives, in addition to the qualifications necessary to the elector, must be twenty-five years of age; and the senators must have resided in the state two years, and must be thirty years of age. The governor must be thirty years of age, an inhabitant of the state four years, and a citizen of the United States twelve years,—he is eligible only for six years in eight.

Notwithstanding the numerous religious sects that are to be found in this country, there is nothing like sectarian animosity prevailing. This is to be attributed to the ministers of religion being paid as they deserve, and no one class of people being taxed to support the religious tenets of another.

The farmers of this state are by no means religious, in a doctrinal sense; on the contrary, they appear indifferent on matters of this nature. The girls *sometimes* go to church, which here, as in all Christian countries, is equivalent to the bazaars of Smyrna and Bagdad; and as the girls go, their "dads" must pay the parson. The Methodists are very zealous, and have frequent "revivals" and "camp-meetings." I was at two of the latter assemblages, one in Kentucky, and the other in Ohio. I shall endeavour to convey some idea of this extraordinary species of religious festival.

To the right of Cheriot, which lies in a westerly direction, about ten miles from Cincinnati, under the shade of tall oak and elm trees, the camp was pitched in a quadrangular form. Three sides were occupied by tents for the congregation, and the fourth by booths for the preachers. A little in advance before the booths was erected a platform for the performing preacher, and at the foot of this, inclosed by forms, was a species of sanctuary, called "the penitents' pen." People of every denomination might be seen here, allured by various motives. The girls, dressed in all colours of the rainbow, congregated to display their persons and costumes; the young men came to see the girls, and considered it a sort of "frolic;" and the old women, induced by fanaticism, and other motives, assembled in large numbers, and waited with patience for the proper season of repentance. At the intervals between the "preachments," the young married and unmarried women promenaded round the tents, and their smiling faces formed a striking contrast to the demure countenances of their more experienced sisters, who, according to their age or temperament, descanted on the folly, or condemned the sinfulness of such conduct. Some of those old dames, I was informed, were decoy birds, who shared the profits with the preachers, and attended all the "camp-meetings" in the country.

The psalmodies were performed in the true Yankee style of nasal-melody, and at proper and seasonable intervals the preachings were delivered. The preachers managed their tones and discourses admirably, and certainly displayed a good deal of tact in their calling. They use the most extravagant gestures—astounding bellowings—a canting hypocritical whine—slow and solemn, although by no means *musical* intonations, and the *et ceteras* that complete the qualifications of a regular camp-meeting methodist parson. During the exhortations the brothers and sisters were calling out—Bless God! glory! glory! amen! God grant! Jesus! &c.

At the adjournment for dinner, a knowing-looking gentleman was appointed to deliver an admonition. I admired this person much for the ingenuity he displayed in introducing the subject of collection, and the religious obligation of each and every individual to contribute largely to the support of the preacher and his brothers of the vineyard. He set forth the respectability of the county, as evinced by former contributions, and thence inferred, most logically, that the continuance of that respectable character depended on the amount of that day's collection. A conversation took place behind me, during this part of the preacher's exhortation, between three young farmers, which, as being characteristic, I shall repeat.

"The old man is wide awake, I guess."

"I reckon he knows a thing or two."

"I calculate he's been on board a flat afore now."

"Yes, I guess a Yankee 'd find it damned hard to sell him *hickory* nutmegs."

"It'd take a pretty smart man to poke it on to a parson any how."

"I guess'd it'd come to dollars and cents in the end."

After sunset the place was lighted up by beacon fires and candles, and the scene seemed to be changing to one of more deep and awful interest. About nine o'clock the preachers began to rally their forces—the candles were snuffed—fuel was added to the fires—clean straw was shook in the "penitents' pen"—and every movement "gave dreadful note of preparation." At length the hour was sounded, and the faithful forthwith assembled. A chosen leader commenced to harangue—he bellowed—he roared—he whined —he shouted until he became actually hoarse, and the perspiration rolled down his face. Now, the faithful seemed to take the infection, and as if overcome by their excited feelings, flung themselves headlong on the straw into the penitents' pen—the old dames leading the way. The preachers, to the number of a dozen, gave a loud shout and rushed into the thick of the penitents. A scene now ensued that beggars all description. About twenty women, young and old, were lying in every direction and position, with caps and without caps, screeching, bawling, and kicking in hysterics, and profaning the name of Jesus. The preachers, on their knees amongst them, were with Stentorian voices exhorting them to call louder and louder on the Lord, until he came upon them; whilst their *attachées,* with turned-up eyes and smiling countenances, were chanting hymns and shaking hands with the multitude. Some would now and then give a hearty laugh, which is an indication of superior grace, and is called "the holy laugh." The scene altogether was highly entertaining—penitents, parsons, caps, combs, and straw, jumbled in one heterogeneous mass, lay heaving on the ground, and formed at this juncture a grouping that might be done justice to by the pencil of Hogarth, or the pen of the author of Hudibras; but of which I fear an inferior pen or pencil must fail in conveying an adequate idea.

The women were at length carried off, fainting, by their friends, and the preachers began to prepare for another scene. From the time of those faintings, the "new birth" is dated, which means a spiritual resurrection or revival.

The scene that followed appeared to be a representation of "the Last Supper." The preachers assembled round a table, and acted as disciples, whilst one of them, the leader, presided. The bread was consecrated, divided and eaten—the wine served much after the same manner. The faithful, brothers and sisters, were now called upon to partake of the Sacrament—proper warning, however, being given to the gentlemen, that when the wine was handed to them, they were not to take a *drink*, as that was quite unnecessary, as a small sup would answer every purpose. One gentleman seemed to have forgotten this hint, and attempted to take rather more than a sup; but he was prevented by the administering preacher snatching the goblet from him with both hands. Many said they were obliged to substitute *brandy and water* for wine; but for this fact I cannot vouch. Another straw-tumbling scene now began; and, as if by way of variety, the inmates of five or six tents got up similar scenes among themselves. The preachers left the field to join the tenters; and, if possible, surpassed their previous exhibitions. The women were occasionally making confessions, *pro bono publico*, when sundry "backslidings" were acknowledged for the edification of the multitude. We left the camp about two o'clock in the morning, when these poor fanatics were still in full cry.

At Hell Town, near this place, there was an officer's muster held about this time. Every citizen exercising the elective franchise is also eligible to serve in the militia. There are two general musters held every year in each county, and several company meetings. Previous to the general muster there is an officer's muster, when the captains and subalterns are put through their exercise by the field officers. At this muster, which I attended, the superior officers in command certainly appeared to be sufficiently conversant with tactics, and explained the rationale of each movement in a clear and concise manner; but the captains and subalterns went through their exercise somewhat in the manner of the yeomen of the Green Island. When the gentlemen were placed in line, and attention was commanded, the General turned round to converse with his coadjutors—no sooner had he done this than about twenty heroes squatted *a l' Indien;* no doubt deeming it more consistent, the day being warm, to sit than stand. On the commander observing this movement, which he seemed to think quite unmilitary, he remonstrated—the warriors arose; but, alas! the just man *falls* seven times a day, and the militia officers of Hamilton county seemed to think it not derogatory to their characters to *squat* five or six. The offence was repeated several times, and as often censured. They wheeled into battalions, and out of battalions, in most glorious disorder—their *straight* lines were *zig-zag.* In marching abreast, they came to a fence next the road—the tavern was opposite, and the temptation too great to be resisted—a number threw down their muskets—tumbled themselves over the fence, and rushed into the bar-room to refresh! An American's heart sickens at restraint, and nothing but necessity will oblige him to observe discipline.

The question naturally arises, how would these forces resist the finely disciplined troops of Europe? The answer is short: If the Americans would consent to fight *à bataille rangée* on one of the prairies of Illinois, undoubtedly the disciplined troops would prevail; but as neither their experience nor inclination is likely to lead them into such circumstances, my opinion is, that send the finest army Europe can produce into this country, in six months, the forests, swamps, and deadly rifle, united, will annihilate it—and let it be remembered, that at the battle of New Orleans, there were between two and three thousand British slain, and there were only twelve Americans killed, and perhaps double that number wounded. In patriotism and personal courage, the Americans are certainly not inferior to the people of any nation.

There had been lately throughout the States a good deal of excitement produced by an attempt, made by the Presbyterians, to stop the mails on the sabbath. This party is headed by a Doctor Ely, of Philadelphia, a would-be "lord spiritual," and they made this merely as a trial of strength, preparatory to some other measures calculated to lead to a church establishment. Their designs, however, have been detected, and measures accordingly taken to resist them. At a meeting at which I was present at Cincinnati, the people were most enthusiastic, and some very strong resolutions were passed, expressive of their abhorrence of this attempt to violate the constitution of America.

Good farms within about three or four miles of Cincinnati, one-third cleared, are sold at from thirty to fifty dollars per acre. Cows sell at from ten to twenty dollars. Horses, at from twenty-five to seventy-five and one hundred dollars. Sheep from two to three dollars. There are some tolerable flocks of sheep throughout this state, but they are of little value beyond the price of the wool, a most unaccountable antipathy to mutton existing among the inhabitants.

Whilst on the banks of Lake Erie, having heard a great deal of conversation about the "lake fever," I made several inquiries from the inhabitants on that subject, the result of which confirmed me in the opinion, that the shores of the lakes are quite as healthy as any other part of the country, and that here, as elsewhere, the disease arises from stagnant pools, swamps, and masses of decayed animal and vegetable matter, which are allowed to remain and accumulate in the vicinity of settlements. When at New York, I met an old and wealthy farmer, who was himself, although eighty years of age, in the enjoyment of rude health. He informed me that he had resided in Canada, on the shores of Lake Erie, for the last fifty years, and that neither he nor any one of his family had ever been afflicted with fever of any description. The district in which he lived, was entirely free from local nuisances, and the inhabitants he represented as being as healthy as any in the United States.

My observations, so far, lead me to conclude, that this climate agrees fully as well with Europeans as with the natives, indeed that the susceptibility to fever and ague is greater in the natives than in Europeans of good habits. The cause I conceive to be this: the early settlers had to encounter swamps of the most pestilential description, and dense forests through which the sun's rays had never penetrated, and which industry and cultivation have since made in a great measure to disappear. They notoriously suffered much from the ravages of malaria, and such as survived the baleful effects of this disease, escaped with impaired constitutions. Now this susceptibility to intermittent fever, appears to me to have been transmitted to their descendants, and to act as the predisposing cause. I have seen English and Irish people who have been in the country upwards of thirty years, who look just as you would expect to find persons of their age at home.

There are situations evidently unhealthy, such as river bottoms, and the vicinity of creeks. The soil in those situations is alluvial, and its extreme fertility often induces unfortunate people to reside in them. The appearance of those persons in general is truly wretched.

The women here, although they live as long as those in the old country, yet they fade much sooner, and, with few exceptions, have bad teeth.

CHAPTER IV

Having decided on visiting New Harmony, in Indiana, where our friend B —— had been for some time enjoying the delights of sylvan life, and the refinements of backwoods-society, T—— and I purchased a horse, and Dearborne, a species of light waggon used in this country for travelling. We furnished ourselves with a small axe, hunting knives, and all things necessary for encamping when occasion required, and so set out about the beginning of September.

We crossed the Big-Miami river, and proceeded by a tolerable road, and some good farms, to Lawrenceburg, a handsome town on the Ohio, within a mile of the outlet of the Miami. From thence we drove on towards Wilmington; but our horse becoming jaded, we found it expedient to "camp out," within some miles of that town. Next morning we passed through Wilmington, but lost the direct track through the forest, and took the road to Versailles, which lay in a more northerly direction than the route we had proposed to ourselves. This road was one of those newly cut through the forest, and there frequently occurred intervals of five or six miles between the settlements; and of the road itself, a tolerably correct idea may be formed by noting the stipulations made with the contractors, which are solely that the roads shall be of a certain width, and that no stump shall be left projecting more than *fifteen inches* above the ground.

On the night of the second day we reached the vicinity of Versailles, and put up at the residence of a backwoodsman—a fine looking fellow, with a particularly ugly *squaw*. He had come from Kentucky five years before—sat down in the forest—"built him" a log-house—wielded his axe to the tune of "The Hunters of Kentucky," and had now eighteen acres of cleared land, and all the *et ceteras* of a farm. We supped off venison-steaks and stewed squirrel. Our host told us that there was "a pretty smart chance of deer" in the neighbourhood, and that when he first "located," "there was a small sprinkling of *baar*" (bear), but that at present nothing of the kind was to be seen. There was very little comfort in the appearance of this establishment; yet the good dame had a side-saddle, hung on a peg in one of the apartments, which would not have disgraced the lady of an Irish squireen. This appears to be an article of great moment in the estimation of West-country ladies, and when nothing else about the house is even tolerable, the side-saddle is of the most fashionable pattern.

From Versailles, we took the track to Vernon, through a rugged and swampy road, it having rained the night before. The country is hilly, and interspersed with runs, which are crossed with some difficulty, the descents and ascents being very considerable. The stumps, "corduroys" (rails laid horizontally across the road where the ground is marshy) swamps, and "republicans," (projecting roots of trees, so called from the stubborn tenacity with which they adhere to the ground, it being almost impossible to grub them up), rendered the difficulty of traversing this forest so great, that notwithstanding our utmost exertions we were unable to make more than sixteen miles from sunrise to sunset, when, both the horse and ourselves being completely exhausted, we halted until morning. I was awoke at sunrise by a "white-billed woodpecker," which was making the woods ring by the rattling of its bill against a tree. This is a large handsome bird, (the *picus principalis* of Linnaeus), it is sometimes called here the wood-cock. Pigeons, squirrels, and turtle-doves abound in all these forests, and my friend being an expert gunner, we had always plenty of game for dinner. The morning was still grey when we set forward.

We forded the Muskakituck river at Vernon, which stands on its head waters, and is a country seat. We then directed our course to Brownstown, on the east branch of White river. We found the roads still bad until we came within about ten miles of that place. There the country began to assume a more cultivated appearance, and the roads became tolerably good, being made through a sandy or gravelly district. In the neighbourhood of Brownstown there are some rich lands, and from that to Salem, a distance of twenty-two miles, we were much pleased with the country. We had been hitherto journeying through dense forests, and except when we came to a small town, could never see more than about ten yards on either side. All through Indiana the peaches were in great abundance this year, and such was the weight of fruit the trees had to sustain, that the branches were invariably broken where not propped.

From Salem we took a westward track by Orleans to Hindostan, crossed the east branch of White river, and passed through Washington. At a short distance from this town, we had to cross White river again, near the west branch, which is much larger than the east branch. We attempted to ford it, and had got into the middle of the stream before we discovered that the bottom was quicksands. The horse was scared at the footing,—he plunged and broke the traces; however, after a tolerable wetting, we succeeded in getting safe out. A little above the place where we made the attempt, we found there was a ferry-flat. The ferryman considered our attempt as dangerous, for had we gone much further into the stream we should have shot into the quicksands in the deep current. This day the fates were most unpropitious to us; and had we had, like Socrates, a familiar demon at our elbow, he most assuredly would have warned us not to proceed. We had no sooner got into the ferry-flat, and pushed off from shore, than the horse tumbled overboard, carriage and all, and was with difficulty saved from drowning.

We passed through Petersburg to Princeton; but having lost the track, and got into several *culs de sacs*, an occurrence which is by no means pleasant—as in this case you are unable to turn the carriage, and have no alternative but cutting down one or two small trees in order to effect a passage. After a great deal of danger and difficulty, we succeeded in returning on the true bridle-path, and arrived about ten at night in a small village, through which we had passed three hours before. The gloom and pitchy darkness of an American forest at night, cannot be conceived by the inhabitants of an open country, and the traversing a narrow path interspersed with stumps and logs is both fatiguing and dangerous. Our horse seemed so well aware of this danger, that whenever the night set in, he could not be induced to move, unless one of us walked a little in advance before him, when he would rest his nose on our arm and then proceed. We crossed the Potoka to Princeton, a neat town, surrounded by a fast settling country, and so on to Harmony.

New Harmony is seated on the banks of the Wabash; and following the sinuosities of that river, it is distant sixty-four or five miles from the Ohio, but over land, not more than seventeen. This settlement was purchased by Messrs. Mac Clure and Owen from Mr. Rapp, in the year 1823. The Rappites had been in possession of the place for six years, during which they had erected several large brick buildings of a public nature, and sundry smaller ones as residences, and had cultivated a considerable quantity of land in the immediate vicinity of the town. Mr. Owen intended to have established here a community of union and mutual co-operation; but, from a too great confidence in the power of the system which he advocates, to *reform* character, he has been necessitated to abandon that design at present.

Harmony must have been certainly a desirable residence when it was the abode of the many literary and scientific characters who composed a part of that short-lived community. A few of these still linger here, and may be seen stalking through the streets of Harmony, like Marius among the ruins of Carthage, deploring the moral desolation that now reigns in this once happy place.

Le Seur, the naturalist, and fellow traveller of Peron, in his voyage to the Austral regions, is still here. The suavity of manners, and the scientific acquirements of this gentleman, command the friendship and esteem of all those who have the pleasure of his acquaintance. He has a large collection of specimens connected with natural history, which the western parts of this country yield in abundance. The advantages presented here for the indulgence of retired habits, form at present the only attractions sufficient to induce him to live out of *la belle France*.

Mr. Thomas Say, of Philadelphia, who accompanied Major Long on his expedition to the Rocky Mountains, also resides here. He too is a recluse, and is now preparing a work on his favourite subject, natural history. His garden contains a tolerable collection of Mexican and other exotic plants.

Harmony is built on the second bottom of the Wabash, and is perhaps half a mile from the river at low water, the first bottom being about that breadth. Mosquitos abound here, and are extremely troublesome. There are several orchards in the neighbourhood well stocked with apples, peaches, &c.; and the soil being rich alluvion, the farms are productive—so much as fifty dollars per acre is asked for cleared land, close to the town. There is a great scarcity of money here, as in most parts of Indiana, and trade is chiefly carried on by barter. Pork, lard, corn, bacon, beans, &c., being given, by the farmers, to the store-keepers, in exchange for dry goods, cutlery, crockery-ware, &c. The store-keepers either sell the produce they have thus collected to river-traders, or forward it to New Orleans on their own account.

We made an excursion down the river in true Indian style. Our party, consisting of four, equipped in a suitable manner, the weather being then delightfully warm, having stowed on board a canoe plenty of provisions, paddled down the Wabash. The scenery on the banks of this river is picturesque. The foliage in some places springs from the water's edge, whilst at other points it recedes, leaving a bar of fine white sand. The breadth of the Wabash, at Harmony, is about 200 yards, and it divides frequently on its course to the Ohio, forming islands of various degrees of beauty and magnitude. On one of these, about six miles from Harmony, called the "Cut-off," we determined on encamping. Accordingly, we moored our canoe—pitched our tent—lighted our fire—bathed—and having acquired enormous appetites by exertion, commenced the very agreeable operation of demolishing our provisions. We roamed about that and an adjacent island, until evening, when we returned to regale. These islands are generally covered with "cane brakes," and low brush wood, which renders it difficult to effect a passage across them. Cotton-wood, beech, maple, hickory, and white oak, are the trees in greatest abundance. Spice-wood, sassafras, and dittany, are also plenty. Of these a decoction is made, which some of the woods-people prefer to tea; but it is not in general repute. The paw-paw tree (*annona triloba*) produces a fruit somewhat resembling in taste and shape the fig-banana, but certainly much inferior to that delicious fruit. We saw several deer in the woods, and some cranes upon the shore. With smoking, &c., we passed the evening, and then retired—not to bed, for we had none—but to a right good substitute, a few dry leaves strewn upon the ground—our heads covered by the tent, and at our feet a large fire, which we kept up the whole night. Thus circumstanced, we found it by no means disagreeable.

We spent greater part of next day much after the manner of the preceding, and concluded that it would be highly irrational to shoot game, having plenty of provisions; yet I suspect our being too lazy to hunt, influenced us not a little in that philosophical decision.

Whilst at Harmony, I collected some information relative to the failure of the community, and I shall here give a slight sketch of the result of my inquiries. I must observe that so many, and such conflicting statements, respecting public measures, I believe never were before made by a body of persons dwelling within limits so confined as those of Harmony. Some of the *ci-devant* "communicants" call Robert Owen a fool, whilst others brand him with still more opprobrious epithets: and I never could get two of them to agree as to the primary causes of the failure of that community.

The community was composed of a heterogeneous mass, collected together by public advertisement, which may be divided into three classes. The first class was composed of a number of well-educated persons, who occupied their time in eating and drinking—dressing and promenading—attending balls, and *improving the habits* of society; and they may be termed the *aristocracy* of this Utopian republic. The second class was composed of practical co-operators, who were well inclined to work, but who had no share, or voice, in the management of affairs. The third and last class was a body of theoretical philosophers—Stoics, Platonics, Pythagoreans, Epicureans, Peripatetics, and Cynics, who amused themselves in *striking out plans*—exposing the errors of those in operation—caricaturing—and turning the whole proceedings into ridicule.

The second class, disliking the species of co-operation afforded them by the first class, naturally became dissatisfied with their inactivity—and the third class laughed at them both. Matters were in this state for some time, until Mr. Owen found the funds were completely exhausted. He then stated that the community should divide; and that he would furnish land, and all necessary materials, for operations, to such of them as wished to form a community apart from the original establishment. This intimation was enough. The first class, with few exceptions, retired, followed by part of both the others, and all exclaiming against Mr. Owen's conduct. A person named Taylor, who had entered into a distillery speculation with one of Mr. Owen's sons, seized this opportunity to get the control of part of the property. Mr. Owen became embarrassed. Harmony was on the point of being sold by the sheriff—discord prevailed, and co-operation ceased.

Of the many private and public charges brought against Mr. Owen, I shall only notice one. It is said that he invited people to throw up their establishments in other parts of America, and come to Harmony, conscious at the same time that the community could not succeed, and, indeed, not caring much about its success, having ultimately in view the increase of the value of his purchase, by collecting a number of persons together, and thus making a town—a common speculation in America. Whether these were his intentions or not, it is impossible for any man to assert or deny; but the fact is no less true, that such has been the result, and that the purchase has been increased in value by the failure of the community, so that *ultimately* he is not likely to lose anything by the experiment. As to Mr. Owen's statements in public, "that he had been informed that the people of America were capable of governing themselves, and that he tried the experiment, and found they were not so,"—and that "the place having been purchased, it was necessary to get persons to occupy it." These constitute but an imperfect excuse for having induced the separation of families, caused many thriving establishments to be broken up, and even the ruin of some few individuals, who, although their capital was but small, yet having thrown it all into the common stock, when the community failed, found themselves in a state of complete destitution. These persons, then, forgetting the "doctrine of circumstances," and everything but the result, and the promises of Mr. Owen, censured him in no measured language, and cannot be convinced of the purity of his intentions in *that* affair. Indeed, they have always at hand such a multiplicity of facts to prove that Mr. Owen himself mainly contributed to the failure, that one must be blinded by that partiality which so known a philanthropist necessarily inspires, not to be convinced that, however competent he may be to preach the doctrines of co-operation, he is totally incompetent to carry them into effect.

But Mr. Owen has also declared in public that "the New Harmony experiment succeeded beyond his most sanguine expectations." Now what may be his peculiar notions of success, the public are totally ignorant, as he did not think fit to furnish any explanation; but this the public do know, that between the former and the latter statement there is a slight discrepancy.

Some of Mr. Owen's friends *in London* say, that every thing went on well at Harmony until he gave up the management—that is, that he governed the community for the first few weeks, the short period of its prosperity, and that it declined only from the time of his ceding the dictatorship. Now Mr. Owen *himself* says, that he only interfered when he observed they were going wrong; implying that he did not interfere in the commencement, but did so subsequently. These are contradictions which would require a good deal of mystification to reconcile in appearance. All the communicants whom I met in America, although they differed on almost every other point, yet agreed on this,—that Mr. Owen interfered from first to last during his stay at Harmony, and that at the time when he first quitted it nothing but discord prevailed.

Very little experience of a residence in the backwoods convinced Mr. Owen that he was not in the situation most consonant with his feelings. He had been, when in Europe, surrounded by people who regarded him as an oracle, and received his *ipse dixit* as a sufficient solution for every difficulty. His situation at Harmony was very different; for most of the persons who came there had been accustomed to exercise their judgment in matters of practice, and this Mr. Owen is said not to have been able to endure. He would either evade, or refuse, answering direct questions, which naturally made men so accustomed to independence as the Americans are, indignant. The usual answer he gave to any presuming disciple who ventured to request an explanation, was, that "his young friend" was in a total state of ignorance, and that he should therefore attend the lectures more constantly for the future. There is this peculiarity respecting the philosophy propounded by Mr. Owen, which is, that after a pupil has been attending his lectures for eighteen months, he (Mr. Owen) declares that the said pupil knows nothing at all about his system. This certainly argues a defect either in matter or manner.

His followers appear not to be aware of the fact, that Mr. Owen has not originated a single new idea in his whole book, but has simply put forward the notions of Rousseau, Voltaire, Condorcet, Plato, Sir Thomas More, &c., in other language. His merit consists in this, and no small merit it is, that he has collated the ideas of these philosophers—arranged them in a tangible shape, and has devoted time and money to assist their dissemination.

I find on one of his cards, printed for distribution, the following axioms, in the shape of queries, set forth as being *his* doctrine,—not the doctrine which *he advocates*.

"Does it depend upon man to be born of such and such parents?

"Can he choose to take, or not to take, the opinions of his parents and instructors?

"If born of Pagan or Mahometan parents, was it in his power to become a Christian?"

These positions are laid down by Rousseau, in many passages of his works; but as one quotation will be sufficient to establish my assertion, I shall not trouble myself to look for others. He says, in his "Lettre à M. de Beaumont," p. 124, "A l'egard des objections sur les sectes particuliéres dans lesquelles l'universe est divisé, que ne puis-je leur donnez assez de force pour rendre chacun moins entété de la sienne et moins ennemi des autres; pour porter chacque homme a l'indulgence, a la douceur, par cette consideration si frappante et si naturelle; que s'il fut né dans un autre pays, dans une autre secte il prendrait infailliblement pour l'erreur ce qu'il prends pour la verité, et pour la verité, ce qu'il prends pour l'erreur."

None but a man whose mind had been warped by the too constant contemplation of one particular subject, as Mr. Owen's mind has been warped by the eternal consideration of the Utopian republic, could suppose the practicability of carrying those plans into full effect during the existence of the present generation. He himself, whilst preaching to his handful of disciples the doctrine of perfect equality, is acting on quite different principles; and he has his new lecture-room divided into compartments separating the classes in society—thus proving that even his few followers are unprepared for such a change as he wishes to introduce into society, and that he finds the necessity of temporising even with *them.*

Another proof of the variance there is between the theory and the practice of Mr. Owen, may be found in the constitution of his new community. The first article says, that, "An annual subscription paid, of not less than one pound, constitutes *a member*, who is entitled to attend and *vote* at all public meetings of the association." These may be termed the twenty-shilling freeholders of the community.[4] Then follow the other grades and conditions. A donation of one hundred pounds, constitutes *a visitor* for life: a donation of five hundred pounds, *a vice-president* for life: and a donation of one thousand pounds, *a president*, who, "in addition to the last-mentioned privileges," will enjoy many others of a valuable nature.

King James sold two hundred baronetcies of the United Kingdom, for one thousand pounds each; and Mr. Owen offers an unlimited number of presidentships in his incipient Utopia on the same advantageous terms. I by no means dispute that the distinction Mr. Owen will confer on his purchasers may be quite as valuable, in his eyes and those of his disciples, as that conferred by King James; yet I cannot help suspecting, despite of the insatiable yearning the aristocracy have after vain-glorious titles, that few of them will come forward as candidates for his Utopian honours.

FOOTNOTES:

[4]

Since writing the above, I find that the constitution has already undergone an essential change; but Mr. Owen appears to entertain views of reformation very different indeed from our present Whig administration, for he has actually placed both *members* and *visitors* in schedule (A) of *his* reform bill, and at one fell swoop has deprived this most deserving class of all political existence. None but vice-presidents and presidents have now the power of voting.

CHAPTER V

Having remained about a fortnight at Harmony, we made the necessary arrangements, and, accompanied by B——, set out for St. Louis, in Missouri. We crossed the Wabash into Illinois, and proceeded to Albion, the settlement made by the late Mr. Birkbeck.

Albion is at present a small insignificant town surrounded by prairies, on which there are several handsome farms. Messrs. Birkbeck and Flowers purchased large tracts of land in this neighbourhood, for the purpose of re-selling or letting it to English or other emigrants. These two gentlemen were of the class called in England, "gentlemen farmers," and brought with them from that country very large capitals; a considerable portion of which, in addition to the money laid out on purchase, they expended on improvements. They are both now dead—their property has entirely passed into other hands, and the members of their families who still remain in this country are in comparative indigence.

The most inveterate hostility was manifested by the backwoods people towards those settlers, and the series of outrages and annoyances to which they were exposed, contributed not a little to shorten their days. It at length became notorious that neither Birkbeck nor Flowers could obtain redress for any grievance whatever, unless by appealing to the superior courts,—as both the magistrates and jurors were exclusively of the class of the offenders; and the "Supreme Court of the United States" declared, that the verdicts of the juries, and the decisions of the magistrates were, in many cases, so much at variance with the evidences, that they were disgraceful to the country. A son of the latter gentleman, a lad about fourteen years old, was killed in open day whilst walking in his father's garden, by a blow of an axe handle, which was flung at him across the fence. The evidence was clear against the murderer, and yet he was acquitted. Whilst I was at Vandalia, I saw in a list of lands for sale, amongst other lots to be sold for taxes, one of Mr. Flowers'. The fate of these gentlemen and their families should be a sufficient warning to persons of their class in England, not to attempt settling *in the backwoods*; or if they have that idea, to leave aside altogether refined notions, and never to bring with them either the feelings or the habits of a *gentleman farmer*. The whole secret and cause of this *guerre à mort*, declared by the backwoodsmen against Messrs. Birkbeck and Flowers, was, that when they first settled upon the prairies, they attempted to act the *patron* and the *benefactor*, and considered themselves *entitled* to some respect. Now a west-country American would rather die like a cock on a dunghill, than be patronized after the English fashion; he is not accustomed to receive benefactions, and cannot conceive that any man would voluntarily confer favours on him, without expecting something in return, either in the shape of labour, or goods;—and as to respect, that has totally disappeared from his code since "the Declaration."

Mr. Birkbeck was called "Emperor of the Prairies;" and notwithstanding the hostility of his neighbours, he seems to have been much respected in the other parts of Illinois, as he was chosen secretary of state; and in that character he died, in 1825. He at last devoted himself entirely to gaining political influence, seeing that it was the duty of every man in a free country to be a politician, and that he who "takes no interest in political affairs," must be a bad man, or must want capacity to act in the common occurrences of life.

From Albion we proceeded towards the Little Wabash; but had not got many miles from that town, when an accident occurred which delayed us some time. We were driving along through a wood of scrub-oak, or barren, when our carriage, coming in contact with a stump that lay concealed beneath high grass, was pitched into a rut—it was upset—and before we could recover ourselves, away went the horse dashing through the wood, leaving the hind wheels and body of the vehicle behind. He took the path we had passed over, and fortunately halted at the next corn-field. We repaired the damage in a temporary manner, and again set forward.

After having crossed the Little Wabash, we had to pass through three miles of swamp frequently above our ancles in the mire, for the horse could scarcely drag the empty waggon. We at length came out on "Hardgrove's prairie." The prospect which here presented itself was extremely gratifying to our eyes. Since I had left the little prairie in the Wyandot reserve, I had been buried in eternal forests; and, notwithstanding all the efforts one may make to rally one's spirits, still the heart of a European sickens at the sameness of the scene, and he cannot get rid of the idea of imprisonment, where the visible horizon is never more distant than five or six hundred yards. Yet this is the delight of an Indian or a backwoodsman, and the gloomy ferocity that characterizes these people is evidently engendered by the surrounding scenery, and may be considered as indigenous to the forest. Hardgrove's is perhaps the handsomest prairie in Illinois—before us lay a rich green undulating meadow, and on either side, clusters of trees, interspersed through this vast plain in beautiful irregularity—the waving of the high grass, and the distant groves rearing their heads just above the horizontal line, like the first glimpse of land to the weary navigator, formed a combination of ideas peculiar to the scene which lay before us.

With the exception of one or two miles of wood, occasionally, the whole of our journey through Illinois lay over prairie ground, and the roads were so level, that without any extraordinary exertion on the part of our horse, he carried us from thirty to forty miles a day.

We next crossed the "grand prairie," passing over the Indian trace. Although this is by no means so picturesque as Hardgrove's, yet the boundless prospect that is presented on first entering this prairie is far the more sublime—the ideas expand, and the imagination is carried far beyond the limits of the eye. We saw some deer scouring the plains, and several "prairie wolves" skulking in the high grass—this animal is sometimes destructive to sheep. The size is about that of our fox. Most farmers keep three or four hounds, which are trained to combat the wolf. The training is thus—a dead wolf is first shewn to a young dog, when he is set on to tear it; the next process is to muzzle a live wolf, and tie him to a stake, when the dog of course kills him; the last is, setting the dog on an unmuzzled wolf, which has been tied to a stake, with his legs shackled. The dog being thus accustomed to be always the victor, never fails to attack and kill the prairie wolf whenever he meets him.

Within thirteen miles of Carlisle, we stopped at an inn, a solitary establishment, the nearest habitation being more than six miles distant. The landlord, Mr. Elliot, told us that he was unable to accommodate us with beds, as his house was already quite full; but that if we could dispense with beds, he would provide us with every thing else. Having no alternative, we of course acceded to his proposal. There was then holding at his house what is termed an "inn fair," or the day after the wedding. The marriage takes place at the house of the bride's father, and the day following a party is given by the bridegroom, when he takes home his wife. The people here assembled had an extremely healthy appearance, and some of the girls were decidedly handsome, having, with fine florid complexions, regular features and good teeth. The landlord and his sons were very civil, as indeed were all the company there assembled.

A great many respectable English yeomen have at different periods settled in Illinois, which has contributed not a little to improve the state of society; for the inhabitants of these prairies, generally speaking, are much more agreeable than those of most other parts of the western country.

When the night was tolerably far advanced, the decks were cleared, and three feather beds were placed *seriatem* on the floor, on which a general scramble took place for berths—we wrapped ourselves in our cloaks, and lay seventeen in a bed until morning, when we arose, and went out to "have a wash." The practice at all inns and boarding-houses throughout the western country, excepting at those in the more considerable towns, is to perform ablutions gregariously, under one of the porches, either before or behind the house—

thus attendance is avoided, and the interior is kept free from all manner of pollutions.

An abundance of good stone-coal is found all through this state, of which I saw several specimens. Were it not for this circumstance, the difficulty of procuring wood for fuel and fencing, would more than counterbalance the advantages, in other respects, presented to settlers on the prairies.

The average crops of Indian corn are about fifty bushels per acre, which when planted, they seldom plough or hoe more than once. In the bottom lands of Indiana and Ohio, from seventy to eighty bushels per acre is commonly produced, but with twice the quantity of labour and attention, independent of the trouble of clearing. There are two denominations of prairie: the upland, and the river or bottom prairie; the latter is more fertile than the former, having a greater body of alluvion, yet there are many of the upland prairies extremely rich, particularly those in the neighbourhood of the Wabash. The depth of the vegetable soil on some of those plains, has been found frequently to be from eighteen to twenty feet, but the ordinary depth is more commonly under five. The upland prairies are much more extensive than the river prairies, and are invariably free from intermittent fever—an exemption, which to emigrants must be of the utmost importance.

Previous to our leaving Elliott's inn, we witnessed a chase of two wolves, which had the boldness to come to the sheep-pens close to the house. Unfortunately the dogs were not at hand, and the wolves escaped among the high grass. Mr. Elliott positively refused accepting of any compensation in lieu of our supper and lodging: he said he considered our lodging a thing not to be spoken of; and as to our supper—which by-the-by was a capital one—he had invited us to that. We merely paid for the horse, thanked him for his hospitality, and departed. During our journey through Indiana we had invariably to use persuasion, in order to induce the farmers to take money for either milk or fruit; and whenever we stayed at a farm-house, we never paid more than what appeared to be barely sufficient to cover the actual cost of what we consumed.

At Carlisle, a village containing about a dozen houses, we got our vehicle repaired. We required a new shaft: the smith walked deliberately out—cast his eye on a rail of the fence close by, and in half an hour he had finished a capital shaft of white oak.

The next town we came to was Lebanon, and we determined on staying there that evening, in order to witness a revival. They have no regular places of worship on the prairies, and the inhabitants are therefore subject to the incursions of itinerant preachers, who migrate annually, in swarms, from the more thickly settled districts. There appeared to be a great lack of zeal among the denizens of Lebanon, as notwithstanding the energetic exhortations of the preachers, and their fulminating denunciations against backsliders, they failed in exciting much enthusiasm. The meeting ended, as is customary on such occasions, by a collection for the preachers, who set out on horseback, next morning, to levy contributions on another body of the natives.

From Lebanon we proceeded across a chain of hills, and came in on a beautiful plain, called the "American bottom." Some of those hills were clear to the summit, while others were crowned with rich foliage. Before us, to the extreme right, were six or seven tumuli, or "Indian mounds;" and to the left, and immediately in front, lay a handsome wood. From the hills to the river is about six miles; and this space appears evidently to have been a lake at some former period, previous to the Mississippi's flowing through its present deep channel. Several stagnant ponds lay by our road; sufficient indications of the presence of disease, which this place has the character of producing in abundance. The beauty of the spot, and the fertility of the soil, have, notwithstanding, induced several English families to settle here. Their houses are built of brick, and their gardens and farms are laid out and fenced tastefully.

After traversing the wood, we at length came in sight of the Mississippi, which is here about three quarters of a mile broad. There is a steam ferry-boat stationed at this point, (opposite St. Louis), the construction of which is rather singular. It is built nearly square, having in the middle a house containing two spacious apartments, and on each side decks, on which stand horses, oxen, waggons and carriages of every description.

St. Louis is built on a bluff bank. The *principal* streets rise one above the other, running parallel with the river; the houses are mostly built of stone, the bank being entirely composed of that material, the walls whitewashed, and the roofs covered with tin: from the opposite side it presents a very gay appearance. The ascent from the water's edge to the back of the town is considerable, but regular. The streets intersect each other at right angles, as do those of most American towns. They are much too narrow, having been laid down and built on from a plan designed by the Spanish commandant, previous to the Missouri territory becoming part of the United States. The population is estimated at six thousand, composed of Creole-French, Irish, and Americans.

St. Louis must, at some future period, become decidedly the most important town in the western country, from its local and relative situation. It is seated on the most favourable point below the mouths of two noble rivers, the Missouri and the Illinois,[5] having at its back an immense tract of fertile country, and open and easy communication with the finest parts of the western and north-western territories. These advantages, added to the constant and uninterrupted intercourse which it enjoys with the southern ports, must ultimately make St. Louis a town of wealth and magnitude.

We visited General Clarke's museum, which chiefly contains Indian costumes and implements of war, with some minerals and fossils, a portion of which he collected while on the expedition to the Rocky mountains with Lewis; and also, two sods of good black turf, from the bogs of Allen, in Ireland. A sight which was quite exhilarating, and reminded me so strongly of the fine odour which exhales from the products of illicit distillation, that guagers and potteen, like the phantoms of hallucination, were presenting themselves continually to my imagination for the remainder of that day.

General Clarke is a tall, robust, grey-headed old man, with beetle-brows, and uncouthly aspect: his countenance is expressive of anything but intelligence; and his celebrity is said to have been gained principally by his having been the *companion* of Lewis to the Rocky mountains.

The country around St. Louis is principally prairie, and the soil luxuriant. There are many excellent farms, and some fine herds of cattle, in the neighbourhood: yet the supply of produce seems to be insufficient, as considerable quantities are imported annually from Louisville and Cincinnati. The principal lots of ground in and near the town are at the disposal of some five or six individuals, who, having thus created a monopoly, keep up the price. This, added to the little inducement held out to farming people in a slave state, where no man can work himself without losing *caste*, has mainly contributed to retard the increase of population and prosperity in the neighbourhood of St. Louis.

There are two fur companies established here. The expeditions depart early in spring, and generally return late in autumn. This trade is very profitable. A person who is at present at the head of one of those companies, was five years ago a bankrupt, and is now considered wealthy. He bears the character of being a regular Yankee; and if the never giving a direct answer to a plain question constitutes a Yankee, he is one most decidedly. We had some intention of crossing to Santa Fé, in New Mexico, and we accordingly waited on him for the purpose of making some inquiries relative to the departure of the caravans; but to any of the plain questions we asked, we could not get a satisfactory answer,—at length, becoming tired of hedge-fighting, we departed, with quite as much information as we had before the interview.

A trapping expedition is being fitted out for the Rocky mountains, on an extensive scale. The number of persons intended to be employed on this, is about two hundred. Teams for the transportation of merchandize and luggage are preparing, which is an accommodation never enjoyed before by trappers, as pack-horses have always hitherto been substituted. These waggons may also be found useful as *barricades*, in case of an attack from the Indians. The expedition will be absent two or three years.

A trade with Santa Fé is also established. In the Spanish country the traders receive, in exchange for dry goods and merchandize of every description, specie, principally; which makes money much more plentiful here than in any other town in the western country.

The caravans generally strike away, near the head waters of the Arkansas and Red rivers, to the south-west, close to the foot of the Rocky mountains—travelling above a thousand miles through the Indian country before they reach the Mexican boundary. These journeys are long and tedious, and require men of nerve and muscle to undertake them; the morasses and rivers which they have to cross—the extensive prairies and savannahs they have to traverse, and the dense forests to penetrate, are sufficient to subdue any but iron constitutions.

The countries west of the Mississippi are likely to be greatly enriched by the trade with Mexico; as, in addition to the vast quantities of valuable merchandize procured from that country, specie to a very large amount is put in circulation, which to a new country is of incalculable advantage. The party which lately returned to Fayette in Missouri, brought 200,000 dollars in specie.

The lead-mines of Galena and Potosi inundate St. Louis with that metal. The latter mines are extensive, consisting of forty in number, and are situated near the head of Big-river, which flows into the Merrimac: a water transportation is thus effected to the Mississippi, eighteen miles below St. Louis. This, however, is only in the spring and fall, as at other seasons the Merrimac is not navigable for common-sized boats, at a greater distance than fifty miles from its mouth. The Merrimac is upwards of 200 miles in length, and at its outlet it is about 200 yards in breadth.

The principal buildings in St. Louis are, the government-house, the theatre, the bank of the United States, and three or four Catholic and Protestant churches. The Catholic is the prevalent religion. There are two newspapers published here. Cafés, billiard tables, dancing houses, &c., are in abundance.

The inhabitants of St. Louis more resemble Europeans in their manners and habits than any other people I met with in the west. The more wealthy people generally spend some time in New Orleans every year, which makes them much more sociable, and much less *brusque* than their neighbours.

We visited Florissant, a French village, containing a convent and a young ladies' seminary. The country about this place pleased us much. We passed many fine farms—through open woodlands, which have much the appearance of domains—and across large tracts of sumach, the leaves of which at this season are no longer green, but have assumed a rich crimson hue. The Indians use these leaves as provision for the pipe.

We stayed for eight days at a small village on the banks of the Mississippi, about six miles below St. Louis, and four above Jefferson barracks, called Carondalet, or, *en badinage, "vide poche."* The inhabitants are nearly all Creole-French, and speak a miserable *patois*. The same love of pleasure which, with bravery, characterizes the French people in Europe, also distinguishes their descendants in Carondalet. Every Saturday night *les garcons et les filles* meet to dance quadrilles. The girls dance well, and on these occasions they dress tastefully. These villagers live well, dress well, and dance well, but have miserable-looking habitations; the house of a Frenchman being always a secondary consideration. At one of those balls I observed a very pretty girl surrounded by gay young Frenchmen, with whom she was flirting in a style that would not have disgraced a belle from the *Faubourg St. Denis*, and turning to my neighbour, I asked him who she was; he replied, "Elle s'appelle Louise Constant, monsieur,—c'est la rose de village." Coulda peasant of any other nation have expressed himself so prettily, or have been gallant with such a grace?

Accompanied by our landlord, we visited Jefferson barracks. The officer to whom we had an introduction not being *chez-lui* at that time, we were introduced to some other officers by our host, who united in his single person the triple capacity of squire, or magistrate, newspaper proprietor, and tavern-keeper. The officers, as may be expected, are men from every quarter of the Union, whose manners necessarily vary and partake of the character of their several states.

The barracks stand on the bluffs of the Mississippi, and, with the river's bank, they form a parallelogram—the buildings are on three sides, and the fourth opens to the river; the descent from the extremity of the area to the water's edge is planted with trees, and the whole has a picturesque effect. These buildings have been almost entirely erected by the soldiers, who are compelled to work from morning till night at every kind of laborious employment. This arrangement has saved the state much money; yet the propriety of employing soldiers altogether in this manner is very questionable. Desertions are frequent, and the punishment hitherto inflicted for that crime has been flogging; but Jackson declares now that shooting must be resorted to. The soldiers are obliged to be servilely respectful to the officers, *pulling off* the undress cap at their approach. This species of discipline may be pronounced inconsistent with the institutions of the country, yet when we come to consider the materials of which an *American* regular regiment is composed, we shall find the difficulty of producing order and regularity in such a body much greater than at first view might be apprehended. In this country any man who wishes to work may employ himself profitably, consequently all those who sell their liberty by enlisting must be the very dregs of society—men without either character or industry—drunkards, thieves, and culprits who by flight have escaped the penitentiary, and enlisted under the impression that the life of a soldier was one of idleness; in which they have been most grievously mistaken. When we take these facts into consideration, the difficulty of managing a set of such fellows will appear more than a little. Yet unquestionably there are individuals among the officers whose bearing is calculated to inspire any thing but that respect which they so scrupulously exact, and without which they declare it would be impossible to command. The drillings take place on Sundays.

Near Carondalet we visited two slave-holders, who employed slaves in agriculture; which practice experience has shewn in every instance to be unprofitable. One had thirteen; and yet every thing about his house rather indicated poverty than affluence. These slaves lived in a hut, among the outhouses, about twelve feet square—men, women, and children; and in every respect were fully as miserable and degraded in condition as the unfortunate wretches who reside in the lanes and alleys of St. Giles' and Spitalfields, with this exception, that *they* were well fed. The other slave-holder, brother of the former, lived much in the same manner;—but it is necessary to observe that both these persons were hunters, and that hunters have nothing good in their houses but dogs and venison.

T—— having gone on a hunting excursion with our host, and some of his friends, B—— and I drove the ladies to the plantation of the latter gentleman. He had a farm on the bluffs, which was broken and irregular, as is always the case in those situations. Large holes, called "sink-holes," are numerous along these banks; the shape of them is precisely that of an inverted cone, through the apex of which the water sinks, and works its way into the river. Cedar trees grow on the rocks, and the scenery is in many places extremely grand. Wild-geese congregate in multitudes on the islands in the Mississippi, and at night send forth the most wild and piercing cries.

Our hostess was one of those sylvan Amazons who could handle any thing, from the hunting-knife to the ponderous axe; and she dressed in the true sylph-like costume of the backwoods. Her *robe*, which appeared to be the only garment with which she encumbered herself, fitted her, as they say at sea, "like a purser's shirt on a handspike," and looked for all the world like an inverted sack, with appropriate apertures cut for head and arms; she wore shoes, in compliment to her guests—her hair hung about her shoulders in true Indian style; and altogether she was a genuine sample of backwoods' civilization. We were placed in a good bed—the state-bed of course—and as we lay, paid our devotions to Urania, and contemplated the beauties of the starry firmament, through an aperture in the roof which would have admitted a jackass.

The proprietor assured us that his slaves produced him no more than the bare interest of the money invested in their purchase, and that he was a slave-holder not from choice, but because it was the prevailing practice of the country. He said he had two handsome Mulatto girls hired out at the barracks for six dollars per month each.

In St. Louis there were seven Indian chiefs, hostages from the Ioway nation. Their features were handsome—with one exception, they had all aquiline noses—they were tall and finely proportioned, and altogether as fine-looking fellows as I ever saw. The colour of these Indians was much redder than that of any others I had seen; their heads were shaven, with the exception of a small stripe, extending from the centre of the crown back to the *organ of philoprogenitiveness*—the gallant scalping-lock—which was decorated with feathers so as somewhat to resemble the crest of a Greek or Roman helmet. Their bodies were uncovered from the waist upwards, except when they wore blankets, a modern substitute for the buffalo-robe, which they commonly wore over the left shoulder, leaving the right arm and breast bare. The Ioways are a nation dwelling in the Missouri territory, and these hostages delivered themselves up pending the investigation of an affray that had taken place between their people and the backwoodsmen.

The day previous to our departure from St. Louis, the investigation took place in the Museum, which is also the office of Indian affairs. There were upwards of twenty Indians present, including the hostages. The charge made against these unfortunate people and on which they had been obliged to come six or seven hundred miles, to stand their trial before *white judges*, was, "that the Ioways had come down on the white territory—killed the cattle, and attacked the settlers, by which attack four citizens lost their lives." The principal chief implicated in the affair, named "Big-neck," was called upon for his defence. In the person of this man there was nothing remarkable. He advanced into the centre of the room, and disengaging his right arm from the blanket, shook hands with the judges, and then, in succession, with all the officers of the court. This ceremony being ended, he paused, and drawing himself up to his full height, extended his arm forward towards the judge, and inclining his head a little in the same direction, said, "If I had done that of which my white brother accuses me, I would not stand here now. The words of my red-headed father (General Clarke) have passed through both my ears, and I have remembered them. I am accused, and I am not guilty." (The interpreter translated each sentence as it was delivered, and gave it as nearly verbatim as possible—observe, the pronoun I is here used figuratively, for *his party, and for the tribe*). "I thought I would come down to see my red-headed father, to hold a talk with him.—I come across the line (boundary)—I see the cattle of my white brother dead—I see the Sauk kill them in great numbers—I said that there would be trouble—I turn to go to my village—I find I have no provisions—I say, let us go down to our white brother, and trade our powder and shot for a little—I do so, and again turn upon my tracks, until I reach my village."—He here paused, and looking sternly down the room, to where two Sauks sat, pointed his finger at them and said, "The Sauk, who always tells lie of me, goes to my white brother and says—the Ioway has killed your cattle. When the lie (the Sauk) had talked thus to my white brother, he comes, thirty, up to my village—we hear our brother is coming—we are glad, and leave our cabins to tell him he is welcome—but while I shake hands with my white brother," he said, pointing to his forehead, "my white brother shoots me through the head—my best chief—three of my young men, a squaw and his[6] child. We come from our huts unarmed—even without our blankets—and yet, while I shake hands with my white brother, he shoots me down—my best chief. My young men within, hear me shot—they rush out—they fire on my white brother—he falls, four—my people fly to the woods without their rifles." He then stated that four more Indians died in the forest of cold and starvation, fearing to return to their villages, and being without either blankets or guns. At length returning, and finding that their "great chiefs" had delivered themselves up, he came to stand his trial.

The next person called was an old chief, named "Pumpkin," who corroborated the testimony of "Big-Neck," but had not been with the party when the Sauks were seen killing the cattle. When he came to that part of the story where the Indian comes from his wig-wam to meet the white man, he said, nearly in the same words used by Big-neck, "While I shake hands with my white brother, my white brother shoots me down—my best chief"—he here paused, and lifting his eyes above the heads of the auditors, his lip curling a little, but resuming again, almost immediately, its natural position, he pronounced in a low but distinct guttural tone, the Indian word meaning "*my* son." His eye seemed fixed for a few seconds, and then, as if conscious of his weakness, and that the eyes of the great warriors of his tribe were upon him, he looked slowly round in a kind of solemn triumph, and resumed his tale. There was a strong feeling excited in the court by the misfortune of this old man, for the "best chief" of the Ioways was his *only* son. The court asked the chiefs what they thought should be done in the matter? They spoke a few words to each other, and then answered promptly, that all they required was, that their white brother should be brought down also, and confronted with them. The prisoners were set at liberty on their parole.

Nothing could have been more respectable than the silence and gravity of the Indians during the investigation. The hostages particularly, were really imposing in their appearance; an air of solemnity overspread their manly countenances, whilst their eyes bespoke that unquailing spirit which the habits and vicissitudes of a sylvan life are calculated rather to raise than depress. The Indians, when uncontaminated by the vices of the whites, are really a fine people; and it is melancholy to reflect that in a few centuries the red-man will be known only by name, for his total extinction seems almost inevitable.

The upshot of this affair proved that the Indians' statement was correct, and a few presents was then thought sufficient to compensate the tribe for this most unwarrantable outrage.

The fact of the prisoners being set free on their parole, proves the high character they maintain with the whites. An officer who had seen a great deal of service on the frontiers, assured me that, from *experience*, he had rather fall into the hands of the Indians, than of the backwoodsmen.[7] Once, while crossing one of the immense prairies in the Missouri territory during the winter season, this gentleman, Mr. R——, was seized with rheumatic pains, and unable to proceed. His party, consisting only of a few men, had no provisions, nor had they any means of taking him with them, being completely exhausted themselves—he was left on the plains to die. An old Indian chief, of one of the hostile tribes, chanced to find him; he carried him home, and nourished him until he was sufficiently recovered to eat with the warriors; when they came to the hut of his host, in order as they said to do honour to the unfortunate white chief. He remained in their village for two months; at the expiration of which time, being sufficiently recovered, they conducted him to the frontiers, took their leave, and retired.

Clements Burleigh, who resided thirty years in the United States, says, in his "Advice to Emigrants," "It may be objected by some that it is dangerous to go to the frontier country, on account of the Indians, wild beasts, &c.; this is no more than a scarecrow. Indians in time of peace are perfectly inoffensive, and every dependence may be placed on them. If you call at their huts, you are invited to partake of what they have—they even will divide with you the last morsel they have, if they were starving themselves; and while you remain with them you are perfectly safe, as every individual of them would lose his life in your defence. This unfortunate portion of the human race has not been treated with that degree of justice and tenderness which people calling themselves Christians ought to have exercised towards them. Their lands have been forcibly taken from them in many instances without rendering them a compensation; and in their wars with the people of the United States, the most shocking cruelties have been exercised towards them. I myself fought against them in two campaigns, and was witness to scenes a repetition of which would chill the blood, and be only a monument of disgrace to people of my own colour.

"Being in the neighbourhood of the Indians during the time of peace, need not alarm the emigrant, as the Indian will not be as dangerous to him as idle vagabonds that roam the woods and hunt. He has more to dread from these people of his own colour than from the Indians."

FOOTNOTES:

[5]

Eighteen miles below the mouth of the Missouri, and thirty-six below that of the Illinois.

[6]

In the Indian tongue there is no distinction of masculine or feminine gender, but simply of animate and inanimate beings.

[7]

"The freedom of manners, and the uncertainty of life, from the various hazards to which it is inevitably exposed, imparts to the character of savages a species of liberality, under which are couched many benevolent principles; a respect for the aged, and in several instances a deference to their equals. The natural coldness of their temperament, admits of few outward demonstrations of civility. They are, however, affable in their mode, and are ever disposed to show towards strangers, and particularly towards the unfortunate, the strongest marks of hospitality. A savage will seldom hesitate to share with a fellow-creature oppressed by hunger, his last morsel of provisions."—Vide *Heriot*, p. 318.

CHAPTER VI

On our return to Illinois from Missouri, we visited the tumuli in the "American bottom," for the purpose of more closely investigating the form and disposition of these sepulchral mounds. Their shape is invariably hemispherical, or of the *mamélle* form. Throughout the country, from the banks of the Hudson to a considerable distance beyond the Mississippi, tumuli, and the remains of earthen fortifications were dispersed. Those of the former which have been removed, were found to contain human bones, earthen vessels, and utensils composed of alloyed metal; which latter fact is worthy of particular notice, as none of the Indians of North America are acquainted with the art of alloying. The vessels were generally of the form of drinking cups, or ewer-shaped cans, sometimes with a flange to admit a cover. One of those which I saw in a museum at Cincinnati, had three small knobs at the bottom on which it stood, and I was credibly informed that a dissenting clergyman, through the *esprit de metier*, undertook to prove from the circumstance, that the people who raised these mounds and fortifications must have been acquainted with the doctrine of the Trinity. How far the reverend gentleman is correct in his inference, I leave for theologians to decide.

The Indians do not claim the mounds as depositories for *their* dead, but are well aware of their containing human bones. They frequently encamp near them, and visit them on their journeys, but more as land marks than on any other account. They approach them with reverence, as they do all burial places, no matter of what people or nation. The Quapaws have a tradition, that they were raised "many hundred snows" ago, by a people that no longer exists; they say, that in those days game was so plenty that very little exertion was necessary to procure a subsistence, and there were then no wars—these happy people having then no employment, collected, merely for sport, these heaps of earth, which have ever since remained, and have subsequently been used by another people, who succeeded them, as depositories of their dead. Another tradition is, that they were erected by the Indians to protect them from the mammoths, until the Great Spirit took pity on his red children, and annihilated these enormous elephants. Most of the Indian nations concur in their having been the work of a people which had ceased to exist before the red men possessed those hunting grounds.

The numerous mounds, fortifications, and burial caverns, and the skeletons and mummies, that have been discovered in these catacombs, sufficiently establish the fact, that a people altogether different from the present aborigines once inhabited these regions. At what period this by-gone people flourished still remains a matter of mere conjecture, for to the present time no discovery has been made that could lead to any plausible supposition.

De Witt Clinton having paid more attention to the antiquities of America than any other person of whom I am aware, I shall here insert his description of the forts. He says, "These forts were, generally speaking, erected on the most commanding ground. The walls, or breastworks, were earthen. The ditches were on the exterior of the works. On some of the parapets, oak trees were to be seen, which, from the number of concentric circles, must have been standing one hundred and fifty, two hundred and sixty, and three hundred years; and there were evident indications, not only that they had sprung up since the erection of these works, but that they were at least a second growth. The trenches were in some cases deep and wide, and in others shallow and narrow; and the breastworks varied in altitude from three to eight feet. They sometimes had one, and sometimes two entrances, as was to be inferred from there being no ditches at those places. When the works were protected by a deep ravine, or large stream of water, no ditch was to be seen. The areas of these forts varied from two to six acres; and the form was in general an irregular ellipsis; in some of them, fragments of earthenware and pulverized substances, supposed to have been originally human bones, were to be found."

"I believe we may confidently pronounce, that all the hypotheses which attribute these works to Europeans are incorrect and fanciful: 1st. on account of the present number of the works; 2d. on account of their antiquity; having from every appearance been erected a long time before the discovery of America; and, finally, their form and manner are varient from European fortifications, either in ancient or modern times.

"It is equally clear that they were not the work of the Indians. Until the Senecas, who are renowned for their national vanity, had seen the attention of the Americans attracted to these erections, and had invented the fabulous account of which I have spoken, the Indians of the present day did not pretend to know any thing about their origin. They were beyond the reach of all their traditions, and were lost in the abyss of unexplored antiquity."

At the Bull shoals, east branch of White river in Missouri, several feet below the surface of the banks, *reliqua* were found which indicated that this spot had formerly been the seat of metalurgical operations. The alloy appeared to be lead united with silver. Arrow-heads cut out of flint, and pieces of earthen pots which had evidently undergone the action of fire, were also found here. The period of time at which these operations were carried on in this place must have been very remote, as the present banks have been since entirely formed by alluvial deposits.

Near the *Teel-te-nah* (or dripping-fork), which empties itself into the La Platte, and not far distant from its junction with that river, there is an extensive cavern, in which are deposited several mummies. Some tribes which roam this region have a tradition, that the first Indian ascended through this aperture, and settled on the earth's surface.

A few years since, on the Merrimac river in St. Louis county, a number of pigmy graves were discovered. The coffins were of stone; and the length of the bodies which they contained, judging from that of the coffins, could not have been more than from three feet and a half to four feet. The graves were numerous, and the skeletons in some instances nearly entire.

In the month of June (1830), a party of gentlemen, whilst in pursuit of wild turkeys, in Hart county, Kentucky, discovered, on the top of a small knoll, a hole sufficiently large to admit a man's body. Having procured lights, they descended, and at the depth of about sixty feet, entered a cavern, sixteen or eighteen feet square, apparently hewn out of solid rock. The whole chamber was filled with human skeletons, which they supposed, *from the size*, to be those of women and children. The place was perfectly dry, and the bones were in a state of great preservation. They wished to ascertain how deep the bones lay, and dug through them between four and seven feet, but found them quite as plentiful as at the top: on coming to this depth, dampness appeared, and an unpleasant effluvia arising, obliged them to desist. There was no outlet to the cavern. A large snake, which appeared to be perfectly docile, passed several times round the apartment whilst they remained.

In a museum at New York, I saw one of those mummies alluded to, which appeared to be remarkably small; but I had not an opportunity of examining it minutely. Those that have been found in the most perfect state of preservation were deposited in nitrous caves, and were enveloped in a manner so different from the practices of the Indians, that the idea cannot be entertained of their being the remains of the ancestors of the present race. Flint gives the following description of one of them which he carefully examined. He says, "The more the subject of the past races of men and animals in this region is investigated, the more perplexed it seems to become. The huge bones of the animals indicate them to be vastly larger than any that now exist on the earth. All that I have seen and heard of the remains of the men, would seem to shew that they were smaller than the men of our times. All the bodies that have been found in that high state of preservation, in which they were discovered in nitrous caves, were considerably smaller than the present ordinary stature of men. The two bodies that were found in the vast limestone cavern in

Tennessee, one of which I saw at Lexington, were neither of them more than four feet in height. It seems to me that this must have been nearly the height of the living person. The teeth and nails did not seem to indicate the shrinking of the flesh from them in the desiccating process by which they were preserved. The teeth were separated by considerable intervals; and were small, long, white, and sharp, reviving the horrible images of nursery tales of ogres' teeth. The hair seemed to have been sandy, or inclining to yellow. It is well known that nothing is so uniform in the present Indian as his lank black hair. From the pains taken to preserve the bodies, and the great labour of making the funeral robes in which they were folded, they must have been of the 'blood-royal,' or personages of great consideration in their day. The person that I saw, had evidently died by a blow on the skull. The blood had coagulated there into a mass, of a texture and colour sufficiently marked to shew that it had been blood. The envelope of the body was double. Two splendid blankets, completely woven with the most beautiful feathers of the wild turkey, arranged in regular stripes and compartments, encircled it. The cloth on which these feathers were woven, was a kind of linen of neat texture, of the same kind with that which is now woven from the fibres of the nettle. The body was evidently that of a female of middle age, and I should suppose that her majesty weighed, when I saw her, six or eight pounds."

The silly attempts that have been made to establish an oriental origin for the North American Indians, have never produced any other conviction in an unbiased mind, than that the *facts* brought forward to support that theory existed only in the imaginations of those who advanced them. The colour, the form, the manners, habits, and propensities of the Indians, all combine to establish that they are a distinct race of human beings, and could never have emanated from any people of European, Asiatic, or African origin. The notion that climate would be sufficient to produce an essential change in the appearance of any number of individuals, cannot now be maintained; since from the discovery of America, Europeans, Africans, and Indians have inhabited all regions of this vast continent, without undergoing the slightest characteristic change from the descendants of the original stock, who have remained in their primitive locations. The Power that induces the existence of plants and lower animals indigenous to the different sections of the earth, seems also to induce the existence of a race of men peculiar to the regions in which they are found.

The languages of America are radically different from those of the old world; and no similitude can be traced between the tongues of the red men, and those of any other people hitherto known. Jarvis, in his Paper on the Religion of the Indian Tribes of North America, says, "The best informed writers agree, that there are, exclusive of the Karalit or Esquimaux, three radical languages spoken by the Indians of North America. Mr. Heckwelder denominates them the Iroquois, the Lenapé, and the Floridian. The Iroquois is spoken by the Six Nations, the Wyandots, or Hurons, the Nandowessies, the Assiniboils, and other tribes beyond the St. Lawrence. The Lenapé, which is the most widely extended language on this side the Mississippi, was spoken by the tribes now extinct, who formerly inhabited Nova Scotia and the present state of Maine, the Abenakis, Micmacs, Canibas, Openangos, Soccokis, Etchemins, and Souriquois; dialects of it are now spoken by the Miamis, the Potawatomies, Missisangoes, and Kickapoos; the Eonestogas, Nanticokes, Shawanese, and Mohicans; the Algonquins, Knisteneaux, and Chippeways. The Floridian includes the languages of the Creeks, or Muskohgees, Chickesaws, Choctaws, Pascagoulas, Cherokees, Seminolese, and several other tribes in the southern states and Florida. These three languages are primitive; that is to say, are so distinct as to have no perceivable affinity. All, therefore, cannot be derived from the Hebrew; for it is a contradiction in terms to speak of three languages radically different, as derived from a common source. Which, then, we may well ask, is to be selected as the posterity of the Israelites: the Iroquois, the Lenapé, or the southern Indians?

"Besides, there is one striking peculiarity in the construction of American languages, which has no counterpart in the Hebrew. Instead of the ordinary division of genders, they divide into animate and inanimate. It is impossible to conceive that any nation, in whatever circumstances they might be placed, could depart in so remarkable a manner from the idioms of their native language."

M. Duponceau, a Frenchman settled at Philadelphia, who is perhaps one of the first philologists of the age, concludes a treatise on the same subject with the following deductions:

1.—"That the American languages, in general, are rich in words and in grammatical forms; and that in their complicated construction, the greatest order, method, and regularity prevail."

2.—"That these complicated forms, which I call polysinthetic, appear to exist in all those languages, from Greenland to Cape Horn."[8]

3.—"That these forms appear to differ essentially from those of the ancient and modern languages of the old hemisphere."

We intended to proceed direct from the banks of the Mississippi to Edwardsville, which lies in a north-easterly direction from St. Louis, but unfortunately got on the wrong track, an occurrence by no means uncommon on the prairies, and by this casualty visited Troy, a *town* containing two houses, namely, a "groggery," and a farm-house, both owned by the one person. The only resemblance this trans-Atlantic Ilium can possibly bear to the city of the ten years' siege, lies in the difficulty of ascertaining its location; for had we not been informed that here stood the town of Troy, we should have passed through this, as we did through many others, without ever suspecting the fact. Town-making is quite a speculation in the western country; and the first thing a man does after purchasing a few hundred acres of ground, is to "lay off a town lot:" this causes the maps to be studded with little circular dots, and great big names attached to them, which would lead one to suppose the population to be much greater than it is in reality.

From Edwardsville, we proceeded by Ripley and Greenville, to Vandalia, the seat of government of the state.

The prairies had lost much of the brilliant green colour which they possessed when we before crossed them, and they were now assuming rather a burnt appearance. Towards the close of autumn the grass generally becomes so dry as to be easily ignited, which formerly took place by accident, or otherwise, almost every year. The sight must be grand indeed; and we almost regretted that we were not so fortunate as to be in danger of being burnt alive—the sight would be worth the risk. There is a penalty attached to the firing of the woods or prairies, as the plantations are now becoming too numerously scattered over the country, and property is likely to be injured by these conflagrations.

Towards the latter end of October, the season peculiar to this country, denominated the "Indian summer," commences, and lasts for some weeks. At this period, the atmosphere is suffused with a vapour which at a distance has the appearance of smoke, arising as it were from fires in the forest. The air is always calm and mild on those days, and the sun's disk assumes a broad, reddish appearance.

Vandalia is the capital of Illinois, and is seated on the Kaskaskia river, which is only navigable to this point during the "freshets" in autumn and spring. The positions of the capitals are chosen for their centrality alone, and not with reference to any local advantages they may possess.

Illinois is a free state, and its constitution is but a counterpart of those of Ohio and Indiana. The extent is 380 miles from north to south, and about 140 miles from east to west: area, 52,000 square miles, or 33,280,000 acres. The population in 1810, was 12,282; in 1820, 55,211: white males, 29,401; white females, 24,387; slaves, 917; militia in 1821, 2,031. The present population is, according to the last census, 157,575. The increase within the last ten years has been nearly 186 per cent.

This state is better circumstanced than any other in the west. It is bounded on the north by the north-west territory; on the south by the Ohio; on the east by the Wabash and Lake Michigan; and on the west by the Mississippi. The Illinois river is navigable at almost all seasons to very nearly its head waters; and by means of a very short portage a communication is established between it and Lake Michigan. A canal is contemplated between this lake and the Wabash.

The heath-hen (*tetrao cupido*), or as it is here called, the 'Prairie-hen,' abounds on the prairies, particularly in the neighbourhood of barrens. This species of grouse, I believe, is not to be met with in Europe; nor has it been accurately described by any ornithologist before Wilson. One habit of the male of this bird is remarkable: at the season of incubation, the cocks assemble every morning just before day-break, outside the wood, and there exercise themselves tilting until the sun appears, when they disperse. Hunters have not failed to note the circumstance, and take advantage of it.

We were frequently amused with the movements of the "Turkey buzzard" (*vultur aura*). This bird is well known in the southern and western states; and in the former is considered of so much utility that a penalty is inflicted on any person who may wantonly destroy it. It is perfectly harmless, never attacking even the smallest living animal, and seems always to prefer carrion when in a state of putrefaction. Except when rising from the ground, the buzzard never flaps its wings, but literally floats through the atmosphere, forming graceful ogees.

During our journeys across Illinois, we passed several large bodies of settlers on their way to Sangamon and Morgan counties in that state. These counties are situated on the Illinois river, and are said to be fertile tracts. The mass of those persons were Georgians, Virginians, and Kentuckians, whose comparative poverty rendered their residence in slave states unpleasant.

Perhaps there is nothing more remarkable in the character of the Americans than the indifference with which they leave their old habitations, friends, and relations. Each individual is taught to depend mainly on his own exertions, and therefore seldom expects or requires extraordinary assistance from any man. Attachments seldom exist here beyond that of ordinary acquaintances—these are easily found wherever one may go, arising from a variety of circumstances connected with their institutions and their necessities; and thus one of the great objections that present themselves to change with Europeans scarcely exists here. Observe, I apply this remark more particularly to the western and southern states; for the eastern states being longer settled and more thickly populated, these feelings, although they exist, yet they do so in a more modified degree.

The appearance presented by the forests at this season is very beautiful—the trees are covered with leaves of almost every colour, from bright crimson to nearly snow-white; the admixture of green, brown, yellow, scarlet, &c., such as is almost peculiar to an American forest, produces a very pleasing combination.

We again reached Albion, and retraced our steps from thence to Harmony, where we deposited our friend B——; and after having remained there for a few days to refresh ourselves and horse, set forward for Ohio. The weather had now become unfavourable, and the frequent rains and high winds were shaking the leaves down in myriads—the entire of our journey through Indiana being across forests, we were under one constant shower of leaves from Harmony to Cincinnati.

One day while getting our horse fed at a tavern in Indiana, the following conversation took place between the persons there assembled. We were sitting at the door, surrounded by captains, lawyers, and squires, when one of the gentlemen demanded of another if there had not been a "gouging scrape" at the "Colonel's tavern" the evening before. He replied in the affirmative; and after having related the cause of quarrel, and said that the lie had been given, he continued, "the judge knocked the major right over, and jumped on to him in double quick time—they had it rough and tumble for about ten minutes—Lord J—s Alm——y!—as pretty a scrape as ever you *see'd*—the judge is a wonderfully lovely fellow." Then followed a description of the divers punishments inflicted by the combatants on each other—the major had his eye nearly "gouged" out, and the judge his chin almost bitten off. During the recital, the whole party was convulsed with laughter—in which we joined most heartily.

We of course returned by a different route through Indiana, passing from Princeton to Portersville, and from thence through Paoli, Salem, and New Lexington, to Madison. The country about Madison is hilly and broken, which makes travelling tedious in the extreme. From the mouth of the Big Miami to Blue river, a range of hills runs parallel to the Ohio, alternately approaching to within a few perches of the river, and receding to a distance of one to two miles. Below Blue river the hills disappear, and the land becomes level and heavily timbered. There is also another range of hills, extending from the Falls of Ohio to the Wabash in a south-westerly direction, which are called the "knobs:" to the west of these are the "flats;" and from the Wabash to lake Michigan the country is champaign.

Indianopolis is the capital of Indiana, and is seated on the White river. This state averages about 270 miles from north to south, and 144 miles from east to west: area, 37,000 square miles, or 23,680,000 acres. The population in 1810, was 24,520—in 1820, 147,178: white males, 79,919; white females, 69,107;

slaves, 190; militia in 1821, 14,990. The present population is 341,582.

Vast quantities of hogs are bred in the state of Indiana, and are suffered to rove at large in the forests in search of mast. They are in general perfectly wild, and when encountered suddenly bristle up like an enraged porcupine. Their legs are long; bodies thin; and tail lengthy and straight. I was informed that if one of those animals be wounded, its screams will draw an immense concourse of its brethren around it, and that the situation of a person under these circumstances, is by no means void of danger; as they will not fail to attack him *en masse*. We were once very nigh getting into a scrape of this description. Driving along through the forest, we had to pass a tract covered with a thick growth of brushwood—my friend seeing something stirring among the bushes, drew up, and taking it for a deer, called out to me to fire—I stood up in the vehicle, and levelled where I saw the movement, when, lo! out starts a bristling hog, with a grunt just in time to escape with a whole skin.

One night having been accidently separated from my fellow-traveller, I had to stay in a miserable-looking hut close to a creek, the habitation of a backwoodsman. This person's appearance was extremely unprepossessing. The air of ferocity and wildness which characterized his countenance, added to his unhealthy, cadaverous aspect, would have been sufficient in any other country to make one feel unpleasant at passing the night alone under his roof. He resided in this unhealthy situation, because the land was extremely fertile; but stated that every fall some one of his family was ill, and none of them enjoyed good health. Now when we summed up the consequent loss oflabour incident to ill health, the balance of profit seemed to be greatly against bottom land, and much in favour of the healthful prairies.

The farmers use, almost exclusively, the sugar of the maple (*acer saccharinum*) which they manufacture themselves. The space in which a number of these trees are found, they call a "sugar camp." The process of manufacturing is as follows:—After the first frost, the trees are tapped, by perforating the trunk in an ascending direction. A spout of alder is inserted in the perforation, and the sap drips through this conduit into a trough of wood. The sap is then boiled with a spoonful of slacked lime, the white of an egg or two, and about a pint of milk, to every fifteen gallons. An ordinary tree commonly gives four pounds of good coarse brown sugar, which when refined can be made equal to superior lump sugar.

A great portion of the roads through which we passed were mere horse paths, full of stumps, with shrubs entangled across them so thickly, that we were often obliged to dismount in order to cut away part of the impediment. Large trees which have fallen across the road, frequently intercept your passage, and you have no alternative but to lift the wheels of the vehicle overthem.

As we approached Cincinnati the difficulty of travelling became greatly augmented. The rains had cut up the roads into ravines, sometimes full three feet in depth, which, added to the clayey nature of the soil, completely exhausted the horse, and rendered him incapable of proceeding faster than a slow walk, even with the empty carriage.

There are a number of Baptists residing at Cincinnati, who frequently entertain the inhabitants with public baptisms in the Ohio river. At one of those ceremonies, about this time, rather a ludicrous occurrence took place. The baptizing preacher stands up to his middle in the water, and the person to be baptized is led to him by another preacher. On this occasion the officiating clergyman was rather a slight man, and the lady to be baptized was extremely large and corpulent—he took her by the hands to perform the immersion, but notwithstanding his most strenuous exertions, he was thrown off his centre. She finding him yield, held still harder, until they both sowsed completely under the water, where they lay floundering and struggling for some time, amidst the shouts and laughter of the multitude assembled on shore. At length their brethren extricated them from this perilous situation.

FOOTNOTES:

[8]

M. Duponceau adduces the following examples: "In the Arancanian language the word '*idnancloclavin*' means 'I do not wish to eat with him.' There is a similar verb in the Delaware tongue—'*n'schingiwipona*,' which means 'I do not like to eat with him.' To which may be added another example in the latter tongue—'*machtitschwanne*,'—this must be translated 'a cluster of islands with channels every way, so that it is in no place shut up, or impassable for craft.' This term is applied to the islands in the bay of New York."

CHAPTER VII

The weather having become cold and disagreeable towards the latter end of December, I set out for New Orleans. The larger class of steam-boats lay then at Shippingsport, immediately below the falls of Ohio, the river not being sufficiently high to enable them to pass over those rapids. Boats drawing from nineteen to twenty-six inches water can almost at all seasons ply on the Upper Ohio, and during the periods that the large boats are detained below the Falls, they are constantly employed in transporting produce, intended for the markets on the Mississippi, to Louisville, from whence it is drayed round to Shippingsport and re-shipped. Flat-boats are also employed for this purpose, and they are preferred, as they pass over the Falls, and thus land-carriage is avoided.

Louisville is the chief town of Jefferson county, in Kentucky, and at present it is estimated to contain about 12,000 inhabitants, including slaves and free people of colour. The store-keepers here are more wealthy than those of Cincinnati, and their manners less disagreeable. The inhabitants of the latter town being mostly from the New England states, have in their dealings and manners that dry shrewdness which is the true Yankee characteristic. There are also located in Cincinnati some Irish pedlars, who have by all manner of means acquired wealth, and are now the "biggest bugs"[9] in the place.

The public buildings of Louisville are few, and the streets are laid out in the usual style, crossing each other at right angles. It contains a few good brick dwelling-houses, and a number of excellent hack-carriages are stationed near the steam-boat landing. A canal round the Falls, from Beargrass-creek to Shippingsport, is being constructed, which will enable steam-boats of the largest tonnage to pass through; and thus it will open an uninterrupted intercourse between the Upper and Lower Ohio, and the Mississippi. The length of this canal is about two and a half miles, and the original estimate was 200,000 dollars, but this sum has been found insufficient.

At Louisville I took a berth on board a boat for New Orleans. The steam-boats on the Mississippi are large, and splendidly appointed; the interior has more the appearance of a well fitted up dining-room than the cabin of a boat. The charge is twenty-five dollars, for which you are found in every thing except liquors. Meats, fowls, vegetables, fruits, preserves, &c., are served in abundance, and of the very best quality. Here you may see tradesmen, "nigger traders," farmers, "congress men," captains, generals, and judges, all seated at the same table, in true republican simplicity. There is no appearance of awkwardness in the behaviour of the humblest person you see seated at those tables; and indeed their general good conduct is remarkable—I mean when contrasted with that of the same class in England. The truth is, the tradesman here finds himself of some importance in the scale of society, and endeavours to show that he is fully qualified to be seated at the same table, *en passant*, with the most wealthy citizen. No doubt the higher classes have some of that high polish rubbed off by these occasional contacts with their less-civilized fellow citizens; but the humbler classes decidedly gain what *they* lose. All dress well, and are *American* gentlemen.

The Ohio is formed by the junction of the Alleghany and Monongahela rivers at Pittsburg, that town being seated in the fork—its breadth there, is between eight and nine hundred yards. From the mouths of those two rivers it narrows and deepens for some distance; but afterwards, from the accession of the many tributary streams by which it is supplied, gradually becomes wider and deeper, until it empties itself into the Mississippi. The length of the Ohio, following its meanders, is about 950 miles, and it may be said to be navigable almost the entire year, as the water must be unusually low when the smaller steam-boats cannot ply to Pittsburg. The character of this river is somewhat peculiar. But for the improvements on the banks, when you have seen six or eight miles of this stream, you are acquainted with the remainder as far as the Falls—that is to say, any variety that may be in the scenery will occur in any given six miles from Pittsburg to that point. Below Louisville there are one or two rocky bluffs, and the face of the country is somewhat different. The channel of the Upper Ohio lies between hills, which frequently approach the *mamélle* form, and are covered with a heavy growth of timber. Where the hills or bluffs do not rise immediately from the river, but recede some distance, the space between the river and the hill is called bottom land, from the circumstance of its being overflown annually; or having at some former period formed part of the river's bed, which is indicated by the nature of the soil. The bluffs and bottoms invariably alternate; and when you have bluffs on one side, you are sure to have bottom on the other. The windings are extremely uniform, with few exceptions, curving in a serpentine form in so regular a manner, that the Indians always calculated the distance by the number of bends.

"The Falls" are improperly so termed, as this obstruction is nothing more than a gradual descent for a distance of about a mile and a half, where the water, forcing its way over a rugged rocky bottom, presents the appearance of a rapid. Below this the country is of various aspects—hills, bottom-land, and high rocky bluffs; and towards the mouth, cotton-wood trees, (*populus angulata*), and cane brakes, are interspersed along the banks. The junction of these two noble rivers, the Ohio and Mississippi, is really a splendid sight—the scenery is picturesque, and the water at the point of union is fully two miles broad.

The Mississippi[10] is in length, from its head waters to the *balize* in the gulf of Mexico, about two thousand three hundred miles, and flows through an immense variety of country. The section through which it passes, before its junction with the Missouri, is represented as being elegantly diversified with woodlands, prairies, and rich bottoms, and the banks are lined with a luxuriant growth of plants and flowers. Before reaching the Missouri, the water of the Mississippi is perfectly limpid; but, from the mouth of that river it becomes turgid and muddy—flows through a flat, inundated country, and seems more like an immense flood, than an old and deep-channelled river. As far as great things can be compared to small, it much resembles, within its banks, the Rhone when flooded, as it sweeps through the department of Vaucluse, after its junction with the Saone.

From St. Louis to New Orleans, a distance of twelve hundred miles, there are but six elevated points—the four Chickesaw bluffs, the Iron banks, and the Walnut hills. Numerous islands are interspersed through this river; and from the mouth of the Ohio, tall cotton-wood trees and cane-brakes grow in immense quantities along the banks; the latter, being evergreens, have a pleasing effect in the winter season. The windings of the Mississippi are, like those of the Ohio, constant, but not so serpentine, and some of them are of immense magnitude. You traverse every point of the compass in your passage up or down: for example, there is a bend near *Bayou Placquamine*, the length of which by the water is upwards of sixty miles, and from one point to the other across the distance is but three.

The town of "Baton Rouge" is situated about 190 miles above New Orleans, and contains a small garrison;—the esplanade runs down to the water's-edge, and the whole has a pretty effect. Here the sugar plantations commence, and the face of the country is again changed—you find yourself in the regions of the south. For a distance of from half-a-mile to two miles back, at each side, the land is planted with sugar-canes, and highly cultivated. The planters' houses are tastefully built, surrounded by gardens full of orange-trees, flowers, and evergreens, presenting the idea of perpetual spring, which here is indeed the case. The winters are seldom more severe than a mild spring in England. I first came in on this region at night, at the season of planting, when the cast or used canes are burned in heaps on each plantation. The dark turgid waters—the distant fires, surrounded by clouds of white smoke ascending in winding columns to the skies—the stillness of the night, interrupted only by the occasional cry of the pelican or the crane, and the monotonous thumping of the steam-boat paddles, formed a strange combination; and had the days of witches and warlocks not long since passed away, one would have sworn that these gentry were performing incantations over the mystic cauldrons, casting "seven bullets," or "raising spirits from the vasty deep."

The Mississippi is in few places more than from half-a-mile to a mile wide; and were one to judge of its magnitude by its breadth alone, a very erroneous estimate would be formed. It is only by contemplating the many vast rivers which empty themselves into the Mississippi that you can form a correct idea of the immense volume of water that flows through this channel into the Gulf of Mexico. Many of its larger tributary streams have the appearance of being as great as itself—the depth alone indicating the superiority of this mighty river over every other in America; and, considering its length, perhaps over any other in the world.

The great valley of the Mississippi extends, in length, from the Gulf of Mexico to a distance of nearly 3000 miles; and is in breadth, from the base of the Alleghanies to the foot of the Rocky mountains, about 2,500 miles. The soil is composed of alluvial deposits, to a depth of from twenty to fifty feet; and I have myself seen, near New Orleans, trees lying in the horizontal position six or seven feet below the surface. This valley has been frequently visited by earthquakes, which have sometimes changed part of the channel of the river, and at others formed lakes. Those which occurred between the years 1811 and 1813, did serious injury, particularly in the neighbourhood of New Madrid, near the west bank, below the mouth of the Ohio. At several points the bank is sunk eight or ten feet below the surface of the adjacent ground, with the trees remaining upright as before.

New Orleans is seated on the south-east bank of the Mississippi; and, following the sinuosities of the current, about 109 miles from the Gulf of Mexico. The river takes here a right-angular sweep, and the city proper is built on the exterior point of the bend, the *fauxbourgs* extending at each side along the banks. At high water the river rises three feet above any part of the city; consequently, were it not for levées that have been constructed here, and also along the banks of the river for more than a hundred miles, at both sides, above and below, the whole country would be periodically inundated. The fall from the levée to Bayou St. John, which communicates with *Lac Pontchartrain*, is about thirty feet, and the distance one mile. This fall is certainly inconsiderable; but I apprehend that it would be sufficient to drain the streets effectually, if proper attention were directed to that object.

The city extends only half-a-mile back, and, including the *fauxbourgs*, about two miles along the river. The streets, being only partially paved, can never be perfectly cleaned, and stagnant water remains in the kennels at all seasons;

this and the exhalations from the swamps in warm weather, produce that pestilential scourge with which the place is annually afflicted. The mortality here last season (the autumn of 1829) has been variously stated in the public prints at from five to seven thousand, who died of the yellow fever in the space of about ten weeks. This statement, however, is erroneous; as, from information which I received from the sexton of the American grave-yard, and from the number of fresh graves which I saw there, I am inclined to think that the total amount falls short of 2500, out of a resident population of less than 40,000 souls. About 700 were buried in the American grave-yard, and perhaps double that number in that of the French.

The port of New Orleans presents the most extraordinary medley of any port in the world. Craft of every possible variety may be seen moored along the levées, and the markets and adjacent streets crowded with people of almost every nation in Europe, Africa, and America, who create a frightful confusion of tongues. A particular part of the quay is appropriated to each description of craft, and a penalty is enforced for any deviation from port regulations. The upper part is occupied with flat-boats, arks, peeroges, rafts, keel-boats, canoes, and steam-boats; and below these are stationed schooners, cutters, brigs, ships, &c., in regular succession. The levée is almost constantly filled with merchandize; and the scene of bustle and confusion which is exhibited here during the early part of the day, fully proves the large amount of commercial intercourse which this city enjoys.

When Louisiana was ceded to the United States, in 1803, Orleans was then entirely occupied by Creole-French and Spanish, consequently the majority of the habitations and public buildings, are in the French and Spanish style. The cathedral, which presents a handsome façade of about seventy feet, the town-hall, and courts, occupy one side of the *place d'armes,*—these, with the American theatre, the *théâtre d'Orleans,* or French opera house, the hospital, and three or four churches, are the only public buildings in the city. The houses are all flat-roofed, and those in the back streets and fauxbourgs are seldom more than one story high; the practice of building houses in this manner was pursued in order to avoid injury from tornadoes, which occasionally visit the valley of the Mississippi; latterly they have not been of frequent occurrence, although when they do arise, they are extremely violent. The town of Urbana, in Ohio, this year (1830) has been nearly destroyed by a visitation of this nature.

Pharo-banks, roulette-tables, and gambling of all kinds, are publicly permitted; but the proprietor of each establishment pays a tax of 5000 dollars per annum. The *théâtre d'Orleans* on Sunday evenings, is generally crowded with beautiful French women. Every night during the winter season there is a *bal paré et masqué*, and occasionally "quadroon balls," which are attended by the young men of the city and their *chéres amies* quadroons, who are decidedly the finest women in the country, being well formed, and graceful in their carriage. The Louisianians are prohibited by law from marrying with quadroons, although this *caste* is free, and many of them have been educated in France, and are highly accomplished.

In the south, slavery exists in its most unqualified condition, wanting those milder modifications which serve to dress and decorate the person of this ugly fiend. Here may be seen hundreds of animals of our own genus exposed in the public bazaars for sale, and examined with as much care, and precisely in the same manner, as we examine horses. In some of the slave states the law prohibits the separation of families, but this prohibition is little attended to, as the slave has no possibility of coming in contact with any dispensers of justice but the magistrates of the state, who, being slave-holders themselves, instead of redressing his grievances, would be more likely to order him a lashing, for presuming to complain. Many melancholy instances occur here, which clearly illustrate the evils of slavery and its demoralizing influence on the human character. The arguments against slavery are deduced from self-evident propositions, and must carry conviction to every well organized mind; yet from their application being of too general a character, they seldom interest the feelings, and in the end leave less impression than the simple statement of a particular occurrence. During my stay, a Doctor —— came down the river with thirty slaves, among which were an old negro and negress, each between sixty and seventy years of age; this unfortunate old woman had borne twenty-one children, all of whom had been at different times sold in the Orleans market, and carried into other states, and into distant parts of Louisiana. The Doctor said, in order to induce her to leave home quietly, that he was bringing her into Louisiana for the purpose of placing her with some of her children —"and now," says the old negress, "aldo I suckle my massa at dis breast, yet now he sell me to sugar planter, after he sell all my children away from me." This gentleman was a strict Methodist, or "saint," and is, I was informed, much esteemed by the preachers of that persuasion, because of his liberal contributions to their support.

Negresses, when young and likely, are often employed as wet nurses by white people, as also by either the planter or his friends, to administer to their sensual desires—this frequently as a matter of speculation, for if the offspring, a mulatto, be a handsome female, from 800 to 1000 dollars may be obtained for her in the Orleans market.[11] It is an occurrence of no uncommon nature to see the Christian father sell his own daughter, and the brother his own sister, by the same father. Slaves do not marry, but pair at discretion; and the more children they produce, the better for their masters.

On the Levée at New Orleans, are constantly exhibited specimens of the white man's humanity, in the persons of runaway slaves. When such an unfortunate negro is retaken, a log is chained to one of his legs, and round his neck is placed an iron collar, from which project three sharp prongs more than a foot in length each.

The evils of this infernal system are beginning to re-act upon the Christians, who are latterly kept in a constant state of alarm, fearing the number and disposition of the blacks, which threaten at no far distant period to overwhelm the south with some dreadful calamity.[12] Three incendiary fires took place at Orleans, during the month I remained in that city, by which several thousand bales of cotton were consumed. The condition of the slaves on the sugar or rice plantations, is truly wretched. They are ill-fed, ill-clad, and worked in gangs under the superintendence of a driver, who is armed with a long whip, which he uses at discretion; and it is a fact, well known to persons who have visited slave countries, that punishments are more frequently inflicted to gratify the private pique or caprice of the driver, than for crime or neglect of duty.

In the agricultural states, slave labour is found to be altogether unproductive, which causes this market to be inundated:—within the last two months, 5000 negros have been sold here. The state legislature has just passed a law, regulating the introduction of slaves, and commanding all free people of colour, who were not residents previous to 1825, to quit Louisiana in the space of six months. Georgia has enacted a law to the same effect, with the addition of making penal, *the teaching of people of colour to read or write*. The liberty of the press is by no means tolerated in the slave states, as both judges and juries will always decide according to the local laws, although totally at variance with the constitution. W.L. Garrison, of Baltimore, one of the editors of a publication entitled, "The Genius of Universal Emancipation," is now suffering fine and imprisonment for an alleged libel, at the suit of a slavite; and a law has been passed by the legislature of Louisiana, suppressing the Orleans journal called "The Liberal." This latter act is not only contrary to the constitution of the United States, but also in direct opposition to the constitution of Louisiana.[13]

The free states in their own defence have been obliged to prohibit people of colour settling within their boundaries. Where then can the unfortunate African find a retreat? He must not stay in this country, and he cannot go to Africa; and although the British government are encouraging the settlement of negros in the Canadas, yet latterly, neither the Canadians nor the Americans like that project. The most probable finale to this drama will be, that the Christians must at their own expense ship them to Liberia (for Hayti is inundated), and there throw them on barren shores to die of starvation, or to be massacred by the savages!

Miss Wright lately passed through New Orleans with thirty negros which she had manumitted, and was then going to establish them at Hayti. These slaves had been purchased at reduced prices, from persons friendly to their emancipation, and were kept by Miss Wright until their labour, allowing them a fair remuneration, amounted to the prime outlay.

Were it not for the danger that might be apprehended from the congregation of large bodies of negros in particular states or districts, their liberation would be attended with little inconvenience *to the public*, for their labour might be as effectually secured, and made quite as profitable, under a system of well-regulated emancipation. We need only refer to England for a case in point:—after the conquest and total subjugation of the people of that country by the ancestors of the nobility, the gallant Normans, the feudal system was introduced, and remained in full vigour for some centuries. But, as the country became more populous, and the attendance of the knights and barons in parliament became more frequent and necessary, we find villanage gradually fall into disrepute. The last laws regulating this species of slavery were passed in the reign of Henry VII; and towards the end of Elizabeth's reign, although the statutes remained unrepealed, as they do still, yet there were no persons in the state to whom the laws applied. It cannot be denied that the labour of the poor English is as effectually secured under the present arrangements, as it could possibly be under the system of villanage.

I look upon slaves as public securities; and I am of opinion, that a legislature's enacting laws for their emancipation, is as flagrant a piece of injustice as would be the cancelling of the public debt. Slave-holders are only share-holders; and philanthropists should never talk of liberating slaves, more than cancelling public securities, without being prepared to indemnify those persons who unfortunately have their capital invested in this species of property.

As many varieties of countenance are to be found among blacks as among whites. There are Africans in this city who have really handsome features, and whose proportions are just, with strong and finely rounded limbs. On becoming more intimate with the general character of the Africans, I like it better: I find they steal, cheat, and hate their masters; and if they were to do otherwise I should think them unworthy of liberty—they justly consider whatever they take to be but a portion of their own. The policy is to keep them as much as possible in utter ignorance—that their indignation should therefore develope itself in the most degrading manner, is not surprising.

There are two public schools established at New Orleans, which are supported out of the fund arising from five gaming-houses, they paying a tax of 25,000 dollars per annum. These schools are conducted on the Lancastrian system, each having a Principal and a Professor, and the studies are divided into daily sessions. The morning session is devoted to reading, spelling, arithmetic, and English grammar; commences at nine A.M., and closes at one P.M. The evening session commences at three, and ends at five o'clock; and is devoted to penmanship, geography, and the French language. This is the arrangement of the English primary school, which is kept in the Old Poydras House, Poydras-street, in the upper part of the city; and is called the Upper Primary School, to distinguish it from the French establishment, which is kept in the lower part of the city. The English school has an English principal, and a French professor; and the French school, a French principal and an English professor. Dr. Kinnicutt, the principal of the Upper Primary School, is a gentleman of considerable ability, and to his friendly politeness I am indebted for the above information.

The ravages of the yellow fever in New Orleans are immense; but I am credibly informed that many deaths occur here from neglect after the fever has subsided, when the patient is in a totally debilitated condition, incapable of affording himself the slightest assistance. Orleans is generally crowded with strangers, who are most susceptible to the epidemic; and it is decidedly the interest of persons keeping hotels and boarding-houses that such guests should give up the ghost, for in that case their loose cash falls into the hands of the proprietor. I do not mean to insinuate that a knife is passed across the throat of the patient; but merely that it is the opinion of physicians, and some of the most respectable people of the city, that every *facility* is afforded strangers to die, and that in many cases they actually die of gross neglect.

The wealthy merchants live well, keep handsome establishments, and good wines. The Sardanapalian motto, "Laugh, sing, dance, and be merry," seems to be universally adopted in this "City of the Plague." The planters' and merchants' villas immediately in the vicinity are extremely tasteful, and are surrounded by large parterres filled with plantain, banana, palm, orange, and rose trees. On the whole, were it not for its unhealthiness, Orleans would be a most desirable residence, and the largest city in the United States, as it is most decidedly the best circumstanced in a commercial point of view.

The question of the purchase of Texas from the Mexican government has been widely mooted throughout the country, and in the slave districts it has many violent partizans. The acquisition of this immense tract of fertile country would give an undue preponderance to the slave states, and this circumstance alone has prevented its purchase from being universally approved of; for the grasping policy of the American system seems to animate both congress and legislatures in all their acts. The Americans commenced their operations in true Yankee style. The first settlement made was by a person named Austin, under a large grant from the Mexican government. Then "pioneers," under the denomination of "explorers," began gradually to take possession of the country, and carry on commercial negotiations without the assent of the government. This was followed by the public prints taking up the question, and setting forth the immense value of the country, and the consequent advantages that would arise to the United States from its acquisition. The settlers excited movements, and caused discontent and dissatisfaction among the legitimate owners; and at their instigation, insurrections of the Indians took place, which greatly embarrassed the government. At this stage of the affair, Mr. Poinsett, the American minister, commenced his diplomatic manoeuvres in the city of Mexico—fomenting disaffection, encouraging parties, and otherwise interfering in the internal concerns of the country. He appears, however, to have carried his intrigues beyond the bounds of discretion, as they were discovered; and he consequently became so obnoxious to the government and people of Mexico, that Jackson found it necessary to recall him, and send a Colonel Butler in his stead, commissioned to offer 5,000,000 dollars for the province of Texas.

Mr. Poinsett's object in acting as he did, was that he might embarrass the government, and take advantage of some favourable crisis to drive a profitable bargain; or that, during some convulsion that would be likely to lead to a change, the expiring executive would be glad to grasp at his offer, and thereby a claim would be established on the country, which the United States would not readily relinquish. The policy of the British government suffering the Mexican republic to be bullied out of this province would be very questionable indeed, as the North Americans command at present quite enough of the Gulf of Mexico, and their overweening inclination to acquire extent of territory would render their proximity to the West Indian Islands rather dangerous; however, it would be much more advantageous to have the Mexicans as neighbours than the people of the United States.

The Mexican secretary of state, Don Lucas Alaman, in a very able and elaborate report made to Congress, sets forth the ambitious designs of the American government, and the proceedings of its agents with regard to this province. He also recommends salutary measures for the purpose of retaining possession and preventing further encroachments; which the Congress seems to have taken into serious consideration, as very important resolutions have been adopted. The Congress has decreed, that hereafter the Texas is to be governed as a colony; and, except by special commission of the Governor, the immigration of persons *from the United States*, is strictly forbidden. So much at present for the efforts of the Americans to get possession of the Texas; and if the British government be alive to the interests of the nation, they never shall;—for, entertaining the hostile feelings that they do towards the British empire, their closer connexion with the West Indies would certainly not be desirable.

FOOTNOTES:

[9]

A "big bug," is a great man, in the phraseology of the western country.

[10]

In the Indian tongue, *Meschacebe*—"old father of waters."

[11]

I have been informed by a gentleman who has resided in the English West Indian Islands, that he has known instances there of highly educated white women, young and unmarried, making black mothers suckle puppy lap-dogs for them.

[12]

Previous to my leaving America, a most extensive and well-organised conspiracy was discovered at Charleston, and several of the conspirators were executed. The whole black population of that town were to have risen on a certain day, and put their oppressors to death.

[13]

Extract from "The Liberal" of 19th March, 1830:—

"Constitution des Etats unis.

"Art. 1 er. des Amendments.

"Le Congrés n'aura pas le droit de faire aucune loi pour abreger la liberté de la parole ou de la presse, &c.

"Constitution de L'Etat de la Louisiane.

"Art. 6, v. 21.

"La presse sera libre à tous ceux qui entreprendront d'examiner les procédures de la legislature ou aucune branche du gouvernement; et aucune loi sera jamais faite pour abreger ses droits, &c.

"Loi faite par la legislature de l'Etat de la Louisiane.

"Acte pour punir les crime y mentionés et pour d'autre objets.

"Sect. 1 ére. Il et décrété, &c. Que quiconque écrira, imprimera, publiera, ou répandra toute piece ayant une tendance à produire du mecontentement parmi la population de couleur libre, ou de l'insubordination parmi les esclaves de cet Etat, sera sur conviction du fait, pardevant toute cour de juridiction competante condamné à l'emprisonnement aux travaux forcés pour la vie ou à la peine de mort, à la discretion de la cour!!!!

"Sec. 2. Il est de plus décrété, que quiconque se servira d'expressions dans un discours public prononcé au barreau, au bane des Judges, au Théâtre, en chaire, ou dans tout lieu quelconque; quicconque se servira d'expressions dans des conversations ou des discours particulars, ou fera usage des signes ou fera des actions ayant une tendance à produire du mécontentement parmi la population de couleur libre ou à exciter a l'insubordination parmi les esclaves de cet Etat; quiconque donnera sciemment la main à apporter dans cet Etat aucun papier, brochure ou livre ayant la meme tendance que dessus, sera, sur conviction, pardevant toute cour de juridiction competante, condamné; à l'emprisonnement aux travaux forcés pour un terme qui ne sera pas moindre de trois ans et qui n'excédera pas vingt un ans, ou a la peiue de mort à la discretion de la cour!!!!

"Sec. 3. Il est de plus décrété, que seront considerées comme illegales toute reunions de negres; mulatres ou autres personnes de couleur libre dans le temples, les ecoles ou autres lieux pour y apprendre à lire ou à ecrire: et les personnes qui se réuniront ainsi; sur conviction du fait, pardevant toute cour de juridiction competente, seront emprisonneés pour un terme qui ne sera pas moindre d'un mois et qui n'excédera pas douze mois, à ladiscrétion!!!!

"Sec. 4. Il est de plus décrété, que toute personne dans cet état quienseignera, permettra qu'on enseigne ou lera enseigner à lire ou à ecrire à un esclave quelconque, sera, sur conviction du fait, pardevant toute cour de juridiction competante, condamné à un imprisonnement qui ne sera pas moindre d'un mois et n'excédera pas douze mois!!!!"

From the remarks of the same journal of the 23rd March, it would appear that the third and fourth sections of this most enlightened and Christian act have been rejected, as being "*too bad.*"

"Nous avons lu la publication officielle de l'acte intitulé: 'acte pour empêcher l'introduction des personnes de couleur libres dans cet Etat, et pour d'autres objets.' Il est trop long pour que nous puissons le publier, nous en donnons l'extrait suivant.

"1. Toute personne de couleur libre, qui sera rentreé dans cet état depuis 1825, sera forcée d'en sortir.

“2. Aucune personne, de couleur libre, ne pourra à l’avenir s’introduire dans cet état sous aucun pretexte quelconque.

“3. Le blanc qui aura fait circuler des écrits tendant à troubler le repos public, ou censurant les actes de la legislature concernant les esclaves ou les personnes de couleur libres, sera puni rigoureusement.

“4. L’emancipation des esclaves est soumise à quantité de formalités,

“Tous les noirs, grieffes et mulatres, au premier degré, libres, sont obligés de se faire enregistrer au bureau du maire, à Nelle. Orleans, ou chez les judges de paroisse dans les autres parties de l’état.

“Nous voyons avec joie, que la partie du bill tendant à empêcher l’instruction des personnes de couleur, à été rejeté.”

CHAPTER VIII

Having spent a month in Orleans and the neighbouring plantations, I took my leave and departed for Louisville. The steam-boat in which I ascended the river was of the largest description, and had then on board between fifty and sixty cabin passengers, and nearly four hundred deck passengers. The former paid thirty dollars, and the latter I believe six, on this occasion. The deckers were provided only with an unfurnished berth. The steam-boats, on their passage up and down the rivers, stop at nearly all the towns of importance, both for the purpose of landing and receiving freight, which enabled me to visit most of the settlements along the banks.

For several hundred miles from New Orleans, the trees, particularly those in the cypress swamps, are covered with tellandsea, or Spanish moss, which hangs down from the branches so thickly, as to give a most gloomy aspect to the forest. It is found to be a good substitute for horse hair, and is universally used by upholsterers for stuffing mattresses, cushions, &c. The process of preparing it is very simple: being taken from the trees, it is placed in water for a few days, until the outer pellicle has rotted; it is then dried, when a long fibre resembling horse hair is obtained.

Natchez, in the state of Mississippi, is about 300 miles above Orleans, and is the largest and wealthiest town on the river, from that city up to St. Louis. It stands on bluffs, perhaps 300 feet above the water at ordinary periods. It contains nearly 4000 inhabitants, and is decidedly the prettiest town for its dimensions in the United States. Natchez, although upwards of 400 miles from the sea, is considered a port; and a grant of 1500 dollars was made by congress for the purpose of erecting a light-house; the building has been raised, and stands there, a monument of useless expenditure. There are a number of "groggeries," stores, and other habitations, at the base of the bluffs, for the accommodation of flat-boatmen, which form a distinct town, and the place is called, in contradistinction to the city above, Natchez-under-the-hill. Swarms of unfortunate females, of every shade of colour, may be seen here sporting with the river navigators, and this little spot presents one continued scene of gaming, swearing, and rioting, from morning till night.

The ravages of the yellow fever in this town are always greater in proportion to the population than at New Orleans; and it is a remarkable fact, that frequently when the fever is raging with violence in the city on the hill, the inhabitants below are entirely free from it. In addition to the exhalations from the exposed part of the river's bed, there are others of a still more pestilential character, which arise from stagnant pools at the foot of the hill. The miasmata appear to ascend until they reach the level of the town above, where the atmosphere being less dense, and perhaps precisely of their own specific gravity, they float, and commingle with it.

The country from Baton-rouge to Vicksburg, on the walnut hills, is almost entirely devoted to the cultivation of cotton, the soil and climate being found particularly congenial to the growth of that plant. The great trade of Natchez is in this article. The investment of capital in the cultivation of cotton is extremely profitable, and a plantation judiciously managed seldom fails of producing an income, in a few years, amounting to the original outlay. Each slave is estimated to produce from 250 to 300 dollars per annum; but of course from this are to be deducted the *wear and tear* of the slave, and the casualties incident to human life. On sugar plantations the profit is much more on each individual; but the risk is greater, and the deaths are generally calculated at one-third of the gang in ten years: this is the cause why slaves *on sugar plantations* are so miserably fed and clad, for their being rendered less wretched would not make them less susceptible to the epidemic. Each acre of well-cultivated land produces from one and a half to two bales of cotton, and even the first year the produce will cover the expenses. A planter may commence with 10,000 or 12,000 dollars, and calculate on certain success; but with less capital, he must struggle hard to attain the desired object. A sugar plantation cannot be properly conducted with less than 25,000 or 30,000 dollars, and the first year produces no return. The cotton begins to ripen in the month of October—the buds open, and the flowers appear. A slave can gather from 100 to 150 lbs. a day. Rice and tobacco are also grown in the neighbourhood of the cotton lands, but of course the produce is inferior to that of the West Indies.

Occasionally, along the banks of the Mississippi, you see here and there the solitary habitation of a wood-cutter. Immense piles of wood are placed on the edge of the bank, for the supply of steam-boats, and perhaps a small corn patch may be close to the house; this however is not commonly the case, as the inhabitants depend on flat-boats for provisions. The dwelling is the rudest kind of log-house, and the outside is sometimes decorated with the skins of deer, bears, and other animals, hung up to dry. Those people are commonly afflicted with fever and ague; and I have seen many, particularly females, who had immense swellings or protuberances on their stomachs, which they denominate "ague-cakes." The Mississippi wood-cutters scrape together "considerable of dollars," but they pay dearly for it in health, and are totally cut off from the frequent frolics, political discussions, and elections; which last, especially, are a great source of amusement to the Americans, and tend to keep up that spirit of patriotism and nationality for which they are so distinguished. The excitement produced by these elections prevents the people falling into that ale-drinking stupidity, which characterizes the low English.

The "freshets" in the Mississippi are always accompanied with an immense quantity of "drift-wood," which is swept away from the banks of the Missouri and Ohio; and the navigation is never totally devoid of danger, from the quantity of trees which settle down on the bottom of the river. Those trees which stand perpendicularly in the river, are called "planters;" those which take hold by the roots, but lie obliquely with the current, yielding to its pressure, appearing and disappearing alternately, are termed "sawyers;" and those which lie immovably fixed, in the same position as the "sawyers," are denominated "snags." Many boats have been stove in by "snags" and "sawyers," and sunk with all the passengers. At present there is a snag steam-boat stationed on the Mississippi, which has almost entirely cleared it of these obstructions. This boat consists of two hulks, with solid beams of timber uniting the bows. It has a most powerful engine; and when the crew discover a snag, which always lies with the stream, and is known by the ripple on the water, they run down below it for some distance in order to gather head-way —the boat is then run at it full tilt, and seldom fails of breaking off the projecting branch close to the trunk.

We arrived, a fine morning about nine o'clock, at Memphis in Tennessee, and lay-to to put out freight. We had just sat down, and were regaling ourselves with a substantial breakfast, when one of the boilers burst, with an explosion that resembled the report of a cannon. The change was sudden and terrific. Between fifty and sixty persons were killed and wounded. The scene was the most horrifying that can be imagined—the dead were shattered to pieces, covering the decks with blood; and the dying suffered the most excruciating tortures, being scalded from head to foot. Many died within the hour; whilst others lingered until evening, shrieking in the most piteous manner. The persons assembled on shore displayed the most disgusting want of sympathy; and most of the gentlemen passengers took care to secure their luggage before rendering any assistance to the unfortunates. A medical gentleman, who happened to be on board (a Doctor Otis, I think, from Carolina), was an exception. This gentleman—and gentleman he really was, in every respect—attended with the most unremitting care on all the wounded without distinction. A collection was made by the cabin passengers, for the surviving sufferers. The wretch who furnished oil on the occasion, hearing of the collection, had the conscience to make a charge of sixty dollars, when the quantity furnished could not possibly have amounted to a third of that sum.

The boiler recoiled, cutting away part of the bow, and the explosion blew up the pilot's deck, which rendered the vessel totally unfit for service. I remained three days at Memphis, and visited the neighbouring farms and plantations. Several parties of Chickesaw Indians were here, trading their deer and other skins with the townspeople. This tribe has a reservation about fifty miles back, and pursues agriculture to a considerable extent. After the massacre and extermination of the Natchez Indians, by the Christians of Louisiana, the few survivors received an asylum from the Chickesaws; who, notwithstanding the heavy vengeance with which they were threatened, could never be induced to give up the few unhappy "children of the Sun" who confided in their honour and generosity: the fugitives amalgamated with their protectors, and the Natchez are extinct.

Some of the Indians here assembled, indulged immoderately in the use of ardent spirits, with which they were copiously supplied by the white people. During these drinking fits, there is always one at least of the party who remains sober, in order to secure the knives, &c. Hence the Americans derive the cant phrase of "doing the sober Indian," which they apply to any one of a company who will not *drink fairly*. One of the Indians had a pony which he wished to sell, having occasion for some articles, and his skins not bringing him as much as he had anticipated. A townsman demanded the price. The Indian put up both his hands, intimating that he would take ten dollars. The pony was worth double the sum; but the spirit of barter would not permit the white man to purchase without reducing the price: he offered the Indian five dollars. The Indian was evidently indignant, but only gave a nod of dissent. After some hesitation, the buyer, finding that he could not reduce the price, said he would give the ten dollars. The Indian then held up his fingers, and counted fifteen. The buyer demurred at the advance; but the Indian was inexorable, and at length intimated that he would not trade at all. Such is the character of the Aborigines—they never calculate on *your* necessities, but only on their own; and when they are in want of money, demand the lowest possible price for the article they may wish to sell—but if they see you want to take further advantage of them, they invariably raise the price or refuse to traffic.

Hunting in Tennessee is commonly practised on horseback, with dogs. When the party comes upon a deer-track, it separates, and hunters are posted, at intervals of about a furlong, on the path which the deer when started is calculated to take. Two or three persons then set forward with the dogs, always coming up against the wind, and start the deer, when the sentinels at the different points fire at him as he passes, until he is brought down. Another mode is to hunt by torch-light, without dogs. In this case, slaves carry torches before the party; the light of which so amazes the deer, that he stands gazing in the brushwood. The glare of his eyes is always sufficient to direct the attention of the rifleman, who levels his piece at the space between them, and seldom fails of hitting him fairly in the head.

A boat at length arrived from New Orleans, bound for Nashville in Tennessee, and I secured a passage to Smithland, at the mouth of the Cumberland river, where I had a double opportunity of getting to Louisville, as boats from St. Louis, as well as those from Orleans, stop at that point. The day following my arrival a boat came up, and I proceeded to Louisville. On board, whilst I was amusing myself forward, I was accosted by a deck-passenger, whom I recollected to have seen at Harmony. He told me, amongst other things, that a Mr. O——, who resided there, had been elected captain, and added that he was "a considerable clever fellow," and the best captain they ever had. I inquired what peculiar qualification in their new officer led him to that conclusion. Expecting to hear of his superior knowledge in military tactics, I was astounded when he seriously informed me, in answer, that on a late occasion (I believe it was the anniversary of the birth of Washington), after parade, he ordered them into a "groggery," "not to take a *little* of something to drink, but by J—s to drink as much as they had a mind to." It must be observed, that this individual I had seen but once, in the streets of Harmony, and then he was in a state of inebriation. Another anecdote, of a similar character, was related to me by an Englishman relative to his own election to the post of brigadier-general. The candidate opposed to him had served in the late war, and in his address to the electors boasted not a little of the circumstance, and concluded by stating that he was "ready to lead them to a cannon's mouth when necessary." This my friend the General thought a poser; but, however, he determined on trying what virtue there was—not in stones, like the "old man" with the "young saucebox,"—but in a much more potent article, whisky; so, after having stated that although he had not served, yet he was as ready to serve against "the hired assassins of England"—this is the term by which the Americans designate our troops—as his opponent, he concluded by saying, "Boys, Mr. —— has told you that he is ready to lead you to a cannon's mouth—now *I* don't wish you any such misfortune as getting the contents of a cannon in your bowels, but if necessary, perhaps, I'd lead you as far as he would; however, men, the short and the long of it is, instead of leading you to the mouth of a cannon, I'll lead you this instant to the mouth of a barrel of whisky." This was enough—the electors shouted, roared, laughed, and drank—and elected my friend Brigadier-general. Brigadier-general! what must this man's relatives in England think, when they hear that he is a Brigadier-general in the American army? Yet he is a very respectable man (an auctioneer), and much superior to many west country Generals. The fact is, a dollar's-worth of whisky and a little Irish wit would go as far in electioneering as five pounds would go in England; and were it not for the protection afforded by the ballot, the Americans would be fully as corrupt, and would exercise the franchise as little in accordance with the public interest, as the English and Irish who enjoy the freedom of corporate towns. Some aspirants to office in the New England states, about the time of the last presidential election, tried the system of bribing, and obtained promises fully sufficient to insure their returns; but on counting the votes, it was found that more than one half the persons who were paid to vote *for*, must have voted *against* the person who had bribed them. It is needless to say this experiment was not repeated. The Americans thought it bad enough to take the bribe, but justly concluded that it would be a double crime to adhere to the agreement. The bravo who takes a purse to commit an assassination, and does not do that for which he has been paid; is an angel, when compared to the villain who performs his contract.

The usual time occupied in a voyage from Orleans to Louisville is from ten to twelve days, and boats have performed it in the surprisingly short space of eight days. The spur that commerce has received from the introduction of steam-boats on the western waters, can only be appreciated by comparing the former means of communication with the present. Previous to 1812, the navigation of the Upper Ohio was carried on by means of about 150 small barges, averaging between thirty and forty tons burden, and the time consumed in ascending from the Falls to Pittsburg was a full month. On the Lower Ohio and the Mississippi there were about twenty barges, which averaged 100 tons burden, and more than three months was occupied in ascending from Orleans to Louisville with West India produce, the crew being obliged to poll or *cordelle* the whole distance. Seldom more than one voyage to Orleans and back was made within the year. In 1817, a steam-boat arrived at Louisville from New Orleans in twenty-five days, and a public dinner and other rejoicings celebrated the event. From that period until 1827, the time consumed in this voyage gradually diminished, and in that year a boat from New Orleans entered the port of Louisville in eight days and two hours. There are at present on the waters of the Ohio and Mississippi, 323 boats, the aggregate burden of which is 56,000 tons, the greater proportion measuring from 250 to 500 tons.

The people of this country cannot properly be compared with the inhabitants of England; their institutions are different, and their habits and manners must necessarily be dissimilar. Indeed, they are as unlike the English as any people can well be, and many of them with whom I conversed, denied flatly the descent. They contend that they are a compound of the best blood of Europe, and that the language of England only prevailed because, *originally*, the majority of settlers were English; but that since the revolution, the whole number of emigrants from the other countries of Europe greatly exceeded the proportion from England and Ireland. Their temperament, organisation, and independent spirit, appear to bear them out in this assertion.

In England we have all the grades and conditions of society that are to be found in America, with the addition of two others, the highest and the lowest classes. There is no extensive class here equivalent to the English or Irish labourer; neither is there any class whose manners are stamped with that high polish and urbanity which characterises the aristocracy of England. The term *gentleman* is used here in a very different sense from that in which it is applied in Europe—it means simply, well-behaved citizen. All classes of society claim it—from the purveyor of old bones, up to the planter; and I have myself heard a bar-keeper in a tavern and a stage driver, whilst quarrelling, seriously accuse each other of being "no gentleman." The only class who live on the labour of others, and without their own personal exertions, are the planters in the south. There are certainly many persons who derive very considerable revenues from houses; but they must be very few, if any, who have ample incomes from land, and this only in the immediate vicinity of the largest and oldest cities.

English novels have very extensive circulation here, which certainly is of no service to the country, as it induces the wives and daughters of American gentlemen (alias, shopkeepers) to ape gentility. In Louisville, Cincinnati, and all the other towns of the west, the women have established circles of society. You will frequently be amused by seeing a lady, the wife of a dry-goods store-keeper, look most contemptuously at the mention of another's name, whose husband pursues precisely the same occupation, but on a less extensive scale, and observe, that "she only belongs to the third circle of society." This species of embryo aristocracy—or as Socrates would, call it, Plutocracy—is based on wealth alone, and is decidedly the most contemptible of any. There are, notwithstanding, very many well-bred, if not highly polished, women in the country; and on the whole, the manners of the women are much more agreeable than those of the men.

Early in the summer I proceeded to Maysville, in Kentucky, which lies about 220 miles above the Falls. Here having to visit a gentlemen in the interior, I hired a chaise, for which I paid about two shillings British per mile.

A great deal of excitement was just then produced among the inhabitants of Maysville by the president's having put his veto on the bill, passed by congress, granting loans to the "Maysville and Lexington road," and the "Louisville canal" companies. The Kentuckians were in high dudgeon, and denounced Jackson as an enemy to internal improvement, and to the western states. It would appear that the friends of Adams and Clay, had determined to place Jackson in a dilemma which would involve his character, either as a friend to internal improvement or an enemy to lavish expenditure. Accordingly, they passed an unusual number of bills, appropriating money to the clearing of creeks, building of bridges, and making of canals and turnpike roads; the amount of which, instead of leaving a surplus of ten millions to the liquidation of the national debt, would not only have totally exhausted the treasury, but have actually exceeded by 20,000,000 dollars the revenue of the current year. This manoeuvre was timely discovered by the administration, and the president consequently refused to put his signature to those bills, amongst a number of others. He refused on two grounds. The first was, that although it had been the practice of congress to grant sums of money for the purpose of making roads and perfecting other works, which only benefited one or two states; yet that such practice was not sanctioned by the constitution —the federal legislature having no power to act but with reference to the general interests of the states. The second was, that the road in question was local in the most limited sense, commencing at the Ohio river, and running back sixty miles to an interior town, and consequently, the grant in question came within neither the constitutional powers nor practice of congress.

The president recommends that the surplus revenue, after the debt shall have been paid off, should be portioned out to the different states, in proportion to their ratio of representation; which appears to be judicious, as the question of congressional power to appropriate money to road-making, &c., although of a general character, involves also the right of jurisdiction; which congress clearly has not, except where the defence of the country, or other paramount interests, are concerned.

The national debt will be totally extinguished in four years, when this country will present a curious spectacle for the serious consideration of European nations. During the space of fifty-six years, two successful wars have been carried on—one for the establishment, and the other for the maintenance of national independence, and a large amount of public works and improvements has been effected; yet, after the expiration of four years from this time, there will not only be no public debt, but the revenue arising from protecting tariff duties alone will amount to more than the expenditure by upwards of 10,000,000 dollars.

A brief abstract from the treasury report on the finances of the United States, up to the 1st January, 1831, may not be uninteresting.

	Dollars. Cts.
Balance in the treasury, 1st January, 1828	6,668,286 10
Receipts of the year 1828	24,789,463 61
Total	31,457,749 71
Expenditure for the year 1828	25,485,313 90
Leaving a balance in the treasury, 1st January, 1829, of	5,972,435 81
Receipts from all sources during the year 1829	24,827,627 38
Expenditures for the same year, including 3,686,542 dol. 93 ct. on account of the public debt, and 9,033 dol. 38 ct. for awards under the first article of the treaty of Ghent	25,044,358 40
Balance in the treasury on 1st January, 1830	5,755,704 79
The receipts from all sources during the year 1830 were	24,844,116 51
viz.	
Customs	21,922,391 39
Lands	2,329,356 14
Dividends on bank stock	490,000 00
Incidental receipts	102,368 98
The expenditures for the same year were	24,585,281 55
viz.	
Civil list, foreign intercourse, and miscellaneous	3,237,416 04
Military service, including fortifications, ordnance, Indian affairs, pensions, arming the militia, and internal improvements	6,752,688 66
Naval service, including sums appropriated to the gradual improvement of the navy[14]	3,239,428 63
Public debt	11,355,748 22
Leaving a balance in the treasury on the 1st of January, 1831, of	6,014,539 75

Public Debt.

	Dollars. Cts.
The payments made on account of the Public Debt, during the first three quarters of the year 1831, amounted to	9,883,479 46

It was estimated that the payments to be made in the fourth quarter of the same year, would amount to	6,205,810 21
Making the whole amount of disbursments on account of the Debt in 1831	16,089,289 67

THE PUBLIC DEBT, ON THE SECOND OF JANUARY, 1832, WILL BE AS FOLLOWS, VIZ.;—

	Dollars.	Cts.
1. *Funded Debt.*		
Three per cents, per act of the 4th of August, 1790, redeemable at the pleasure of government	13,296,626	21
Five per cents, per act of the 3rd of March, 1821, redeemable after the 1st January, 1823	4,735,296	30
Five per cents, (exchanged), per act of 20th of April, 1823; one third redeemable annually after 31st of December, 1830, 1831 and 1832	56,704	77
Four and half per cents. per act of the 24th of May, 1824, redeemable after 1st of January, 1832	1,739,524	01
Four and half per cents. (exchanged), per act of the 26th of May, 1824; one half redeemable after the 31st day of December, 1832	4,454,727	95
	24,282,879	24
2. *Unfunded Debt.*		
Registered Debt, being claims registered prior to the year 1793, for services and supplies during the revolutionary war	27,919	85
Treasury notes	7,116	00
Mississippi stock	4,320	09
	39,355	94
Making the whole amount of the Public Debt of the United States	24,322,235	18
Which is, allowing 480 cents to the sovereign, in sterling money	£5,067,132 *6s.* *7d.*	

General Jackson has proposed another source of national revenue, in the establishment of a bank; the profits of which, instead of going into the pockets of stock-holders as at present, should be placed to the credit of the nation. If an establishment of this nature could be formed, without involving higher interests than the mere pecuniary concerns of the country, no doubt it would be most desirable. But how a *government* bank could be so formed as that it should not throw immense and dangerous influence into the hands of the executive, appears difficult to determine. If it be at all connected with the government, the executive must exercise an extensive authority over its affairs; and in that case, the mercantile portion of the community would lie completely under the surveillance of the president, who might at pleasure exercise this immense patronage to forward private political designs. No doubt there have been abuses to a considerable extent practised by the present bank of the United States in the exercise of its functions; but how those abuses are likely to be remedied by Jackson's plan, does not appear. For, let the directors be appointed by government, or elected by congress, they must still exercise discretional power; and they are quite as likely to exercise it unwarrantably as those who have a direct interest in the prosperity of the concern. I totally disapprove of the attempt to correct the abuses of one monopoly by the establishment of another in its stead, of a still more dangerous character; and I am inclined to think that if two banks were chartered instead of one, each having ample capital to insure public confidence, competition alone would furnish a sufficient motive to induce them to act with justice and liberality towards the public.

In 1766, Kentucky was first explored, by John Finlay, an Indian trader, Colonel Daniel Boon, and others. They again visited it in 1769, when the whole party, excepting Boon, were slain by the Indians—he escaped, and reached North Carolina, where he then resided. Accompanied by about forty expert hunters, comprised in five families, in the year 1775, he set forward to make a settlement in the country. They erected a fort on the banks of the Kentucky river, and being joined by several other adventurers, they finally succeeded. The Kentuckians tell of many a bloody battle fought by these pioneers, and boast that their country has been gained, every inch, by conquest.

The climate of Kentucky is favourable to the growth of hemp, flax, tobacco, and all kinds of grain. The greater portion of the soil is rich loam, black, or mixed with reddish earth, generally to the depth of five or six feet, on a limestone bottom. The produce of corn is about sixty bushels on an average per acre, and of wheat about thirty-five; cotton is partially cultivated. The scenery is varied, and the country well watered.

The Kentuckians all carry large pocket knives, which they never fail to use in a scuffle; and you may see a gentleman seated at the tavern door, balanced on two legs of a chair, picking his teeth with a knife, the blade of which is full six inches long, or cutting the benches, posts, or any thing else that may lie within his reach. Notwithstanding this, the Kentuckians are by no means more quarrelsome than any other people of the western states; and they are vastly less so than the people of Ireland. But when they do commence hostilities, they fight with great bitterness, as do most Americans, biting, gouging, and cutting unrelentingly.

I never went into a court-house in the west *in summer*, without observing that the judges and lawyers had their feet invariably placed upon the desks before them, and raised much higher than their heads. This, however, is only in the western country; for in the courts at Orleans, New York, and Philadelphia, the greatest order and regularity is observed. I had been told that the judges often slept upon the bench; but I must confess, that although I have entered court-houses at all seasons during the space of fifteen months, I never saw an instance of it. I have frequently remonstrated with the Americans, on the total absence of forms and ceremonies in their courts of justice, and was commonly answered by "Yes, that may be quite necessary in England, in order to overawe a parcel of ignorant creatures, who have no share in making the laws; but with us, a man's a man, whether he have a silk gown on him or not; and I guess he can decide quite as well without a big wig as with one. You see, we have done with wiggery of all kinds; and if one of our judges were to wear such an appendage, he'd be taken for a merry-andrew, and the court would become a kind of show-box—instead of such arrangements producing with us solemnity, they would produce nothing but laughter, and the greatest possible irregularity."

I was present at an election in the interior of the state. The office was that of representative in the state legislature, and the candidates were a hatter and a saddler; the former was also a militia major, and a Methodist preacher, of the Percival and Gordon school, who eschewed the devil and all the backsliding abominations of the flesh, as in duty bound. Sundry "stump orations" were delivered on the occasion, for the enlightenment of the electors; and towards the close of the proceedings, by way of an appropriate finale, the aforesaid triune-citizen and another gentleman, had a gouging scrape on the hustings. The major in this contest proved himself to be a true Kentuckian; that is, half a horse, and half an alligator; which contributed not a little to ensure his return. After the election, I was conversing with one of the most violent opponents of the successful candidate, and remarked to him, that I supposed he would rally his forces at the next election to put out the major: he replied, "I can't tell that!" I said, "why? will you not oppose him?" "Oh!" he says, "for that matter, he may do his duty pretty well." "And do you mean to say," continued I, "that if he should do so, you will give him no opposition?" He looked at me, as if he did not clearly comprehend, and said, "Why, I guess not."

The boatmen of the Ohio and Mississippi are the most riotous and lawless set of people in America, and the least inclined to submit to the constituted authorities. At Cincinnati I saw one of those persons arrested, on the wharf, for debt. He seemed little inclined to submit; as, could he contrive to escape to the opposite shore, he was safe. He called upon his companions in the flat-boat, who came instantly to his assistance, and were apparently ready to rescue him from the clutches of this trans-Atlantic bum-bailiff. The constable instantly pulled out—not a pistol, but a small piece of paper, and said, "I take him in the name of the States." The messmates of this unfortunate navigator looked at him for some time, and then one of them said drily, "I guess you must go with the constable." Subsequently, at New York, one evening returning to my hotel, I heard a row in a tavern, and wishing to see the process of capturing refractory citizens, I entered with some other persons. The constable was there unsupported by any of his brethren, and it seemed to me to be morally impossible that, without assistance, he could take half a dozen fellows, who were with difficulty restrained from whipping each other. However, his hand seemed to be as potent as the famous magic wand of Armida, for on placing it on the shoulders of the combatants, they fell into the ranks, and marched off with him as quietly as if they had been sheep. The rationale of the matter is this: those men had all exercised the franchise, if not in the election of these very constables, of others, and they therefore not only considered it to be their duty to support the constable's authority, but actually felt a strong inclination to do so. Because they *knew* that the authority he exercised was only delegated to him by themselves, and that, in resisting him, they would resist their own sovereignty. Even in large towns in the western country, the constable has no men under his command, but always finds most powerful allies in the citizens themselves, whenever a lawless scoundrel, or a culprit is to be captured.

At Flemingsburg I saw an Albino, a female about fourteen years old. Her parents were clear negros, of the Congo or Guinea race, and in every thing but colour she perfectly resembled them. Her form, face, and hair, possessed the true negro characteristics—curved shins, projecting jaw, retreating forehead, and woolly head. The skin was rather whiter than that of the generality of Europeans, but was deficient in glossiness, and although perfectly smooth, had a dry appearance. The wool on the head was of a light flaxen colour, and the iris of the eye was of a reddish-blue tinge. Her eyes were so weak as to bear with difficulty the glare of day. Most Albinos are dim sighted until twilight, when they appear to have as perfect vision as persons with the strongest sight, and in many cases, even more acute. This individual had evidently weak sight, as the eyelids were generally half closed, and she always held her head down during day light.

Near the banks of the Ohio, full three hundred miles from the sea, I found conglomerations of marine shells, mixed with siliceous earth; and in nearly all the runs throughout Kentucky, limestone pebbles are found, bearing the perfect impressions of the interior of shells. The most abundant proofs are every where exhibited, that at one period the vast savannahs and lofty mountains of the New world were submerged; and perhaps the present bed of the ocean was once covered with verdure, and the seat of the sorrows and joys of myriads of human beings, who erected cities, and built pyramids, and monuments, which Time has long since swept away, and wrapt in his eternal mantle of oblivion. That a constant, but almost imperceptible change is hourly taking place in the earth's surface, appears to be established; and independent of the extraordinary *bouleversements*, which have at intervals convulsed our globe, this gradual revolution has produced, and will produce again, a total alteration in the face of nature.

FOOTNOTES:

[14]

Amongst other plans to this effect, there is one proposed, by which midshipmen on half-pay will be obliged to make at least two voyages annually, in merchant ships, as mates, and all others must have done so, in order to entitle them to be reinstated in their former rank. Another is, that there shall be small vessels, rigged and fitted out in war style, appropriated to the purpose of teaching pupils, practically, the science of navigation, and the discipline necessary to be observed on board vessels of war. The Americans may not eat their fish with silver forks, nor lave their fingers in the most approved style; yet they are by no means so contemptible a people as some of our small gentry affect to think. They may too, occasionally, be put down in political argument, by the dogmatical method of the quarter-deck; but I must confess that *I* never was so fortunate as to come in contact with any who reasoned so badly as the persons Captain Bazil Hall introduces in his book.

CHAPTER IX

The wailings of the Cherokee, the Choctaw, and the Creek, may have been wafted across the waters of the great salt lake, and the Pale-face in his own land may have heard their lamentations;—but the distant voice is scattered by the passing winds, and is heard like the whisper of a summer breeze as it steals along the prairies of the west, or the cry of the wish-ton-wish as it faintly reaches the ear of the navigator, when, in the stilly night, he floats down "the old father of waters."

The present posture of Indian affairs, and the peculiar situation of the Indian nations east of the Mississippi, have caused that unfortunate people to be the topic of much political controversy and conversation; a succinct account of the political condition of these tribes, and of the policy which has been pursued, and which is being pursued towards them, by the executive government, may not therefore be uninteresting.

When Georgia, by becoming a member of the Union, ceded part of her sovereignty to the general executive, that government acknowledged her claimed limits, and guaranteed to her the protection of the Union against foreign and domestic violence. Subsequently, in the year of 1802, in consideration of a certain portion of lands ceded, the United States became bound to purchase for Georgia, any claim which the Cherokee nation might have on lands within her boundaries, whenever such purchase could be made on reasonable terms. On these positions are based the Georgian claims, which the United States government has hitherto pleaded inability to satisfy, inasmuch as all efforts to purchase the Indian lands have proved fruitless.

After the lapse of twenty-seven years, Georgia, finding herself precisely in the same condition in which she then stood, has determined on forcibly taking possession of the Cherokee lands, and extending her sovereignty over the Cherokee people. But as this cannot be effected without doing manifest violence to the Indian rights, she brings forward arguments to show, that *she* never acknowledged the independence of the Cherokee nation; that that nation, from the time of the first settlement made by Europeans in America, stood in the position of a conquered people; that the sovereignty consequently dwelt in the hands of Great Britain; and that, on the Declaration of independence, Georgia, by becoming a free state, became invested with all the powers of sovereignty claimed or exercised by Great Britain over the Georgian territory: and further, that in November, 1785, when the first and only treaty was concluded with the Cherokees by the United States, during the articles of confederation, both she and North Carolina entered their solemn protests against this alleged violation of their legislative rights. The executive government pretends not to argue the case with Georgia, and is left no alternative but either to annul its *conditional* treaty with that state, or to cancel *thirteen distinct treaties* entered into with the Indians, despoil them of their lands, and rob them of their independence. Jackson's message says, "It is too late to inquire whether it was just in the United States to include them and their territory within bounds of new states, whose limits they could control. That step cannot be retracted. A state cannot be dismembered by Congress, or restrained in the exercise of her constitutional powers." Here the executive government acknowledges that it made promises to Georgia, which it has been unable to perform—that it guaranteed to that state the possession of lands over which it had no legitimate control, on the mere assumption of being able to make their purchase.

The Cherokees in their petition and memorials to Congress show, that Great Britain never exercised any sovereignty over them;—that in peace and in war she always treated them as a free people, and never assumed to herself the right of interfering with their internal government:—that in every treaty made with them by the United States, their sovereignty and total independence are clearly acknowledged, and that they have ever been considered as a distinct nation, exercising all the privileges and immunities enjoyed by any independent people. They say, "In addition to that first of all rights, the right of inheritance and peaceable possession, we have the faith and pledge of the United States, over and over again, in treaties made at various times. By these treaties our rights as a separate people are distinctly acknowledged, and guarantees given that they shall be secured and protected. So we have also understood the treaties. The conduct of the government towards us, from its organization until very lately—the talks given to our beloved men by the Presidents of the United States—and the speeches of the agents and commissioners—all concur to show that we are not mistaken in our interpretation. Some of our beloved men who signed the treaties are still living, and their testimony tends to the same conclusion." * * * * "In what light shall we view the conduct of the United States and Georgia in their intercourse with us, in urging us to enter into treaties and cede lands? If we were but tenants at will, why was it necessary that our consent must first be obtained before these governments could take lawful possession of our lands? The answer is obvious. These governments perfectly understand our rights—our right to the country, and our right to self-government. Our understanding of the treaties is further supported by the intercourse law of the United States, which prohibits all encroachment on our territory."

The arguments used by the Cherokees are unanswerable; but in what will that avail them, when injustice is intended by a superior power, which, regardless of national faith, has determined on taking possession of their lands? The case stands thus: the executive government enters into an agreement with Georgia, and engages to deliver over to the state the Indian possessions within her claimed limits—without the Indians *having any knowledge of, or participation in the transaction.* Now what, may I ask, have the Indians to do with this? Ought they to be made answerable for the gross misconduct of the two governments, and to be despoiled, contrary to every principle of justice, and in defiance of the most plain and fundamental law of property? It puts one in mind of the judgment of the renowned "Walter the Doubter," who decided between two citizens, that, as their account books appeared to be of equal *weight*, therefore their accounts were balanced, and that *the constable* should pay the costs. The United States government has made several offers to the Cherokees for their lands; which they have as constantly refused, and said, "that they were very well contented where they were—that they did not wish to leave the bones of their ancestors, and go beyond the Mississippi; but that, if the country be so beautiful as their white brother represents it, they would recommend their white brother to go there himself."

Georgia presses upon the executive; which, in this dilemma, comes forward with affected sympathy—deplores the unfortunate situation in which it is placed, but of course concludes that faith must be kept with Georgia, and that the Cherokee must either go, or submit to laws that make it far better for him to go than stay. It is true Jackson says in his message, "This emigration should be voluntary; for it would be cruel as unjust to compel the Aborigines to abandon the graves of their fathers, and seek a home in a distant land." But General Jackson well knows that the laws of Georgia leave the Indian no choice—as no community of men, civilized or savage, could possibly exist under such laws. The benefit and protection of the laws, to which the Indian is made subject, are entirely withheld from him—he can be no party to a suit—he may be robbed and murdered with impunity—his property may be taken, and he may be driven from his dwelling—in fine, he is left liable to every species of insult, outrage, cruelty, and dishonesty, without the most distant hope of obtaining redress; for in Georgia *an Indian cannot be a witness to prove facts against a white man.* Yet General Jackson says, "this emigration should be *voluntary*;" and in the very same paragraph, with a single sweep of the pen, he annihilates all the treaties that have been made with that people—tramples under foot the laws of nations, and deprives the Indian of his hunting-grounds, one of his sources of subsistence. He says,—"But it seems to me visionary to suppose that, in this state of things, claims can be allowed on tracts of country on which they have neither dwelt nor made improvements, merely because they have seen them from the mountain, or passed them in the chase." It certainly may be unphilosophical to permit any man to possess more ground than he can till with his own hands; yet surely arguments that we do not admit as regards ourselves, we can with no sense of propriety use towards others, particularly when our own acts are directly in the very teeth of this principle. There is more land at present within the limits and in the possession of the United States than would be sufficient to support thirty times the present population—yet to this must be added the hunting-grounds of the Indians, merely because "it is *visionary to suppose* they have any claim on what they do not *actually occupy!"*

I have now before me the particulars of thirteen treaties[15] made by the United States with the Cherokee nation, from the year 1785 down to 1819 inclusive; in all of which the rights of the Indians are clearly acknowledged, either directly, or by implication; and by the seventh article of the treaty of Holston, executed in 1791, being the first concluded with that people by the United States, under their present constitution, all the lands not thereby ceded are solemnly guaranteed to the Cherokee nation. The subsequent treaties are made with reference to, and in confirmation of this, and continually reiterate the guarantees therein tendered.

To talk of justice, and honour, would be idle and visionary, for these seem to have been thrown overboard at the very commencement of the contest; but I would ask the American *people*, is their conduct towards the Indians politic? —is it politic in America, in the face of civilized nations, to violate treaties? is it politic in her, to hold herself up to the world as faithless and unjust—as a nation, which, in defiance of all moral obligation, will break her most sacred contracts, whenever it becomes no longer her interest to keep them, and she finds herself in a condition to do so with impunity? is she not furnishing foreign statesmen with a ready and powerful argument in defence of their violating treaties with her? can they not with justice say—America has manifested in her proceedings towards the Cherokee nation, that she is faithless—that she keeps no treaties longer than it may be her *interest* to do so —and are *we* to make ourselves the dupes of such a power, and wait until she finds herself in a condition to deceive us? I could produce many arguments to illustrate the impolicy of this conduct; but as I intend confining myself to a mere sketch, I shall dwell but as short a time as may be consistent on the several facts connected with the case.

That the Aborigines have been cruelly treated, cannot be doubted. The very words of the Message admit this; and the tone of feeling and conciliation which follows that admission, coupled as it is with the intended injustice expressed in other paragraphs, can be viewed in no other light than as a piece of political mockery. The Message says, "their present condition, contrasted with what they once were, makes a most powerful appeal to our sympathies. Our ancestors found them the uncontrolled possessors of these vast regions. By persuasion and force, they have been made to retire from river to river, and from mountain to mountain, until some of the tribes have become extinct, and others have left but remnants, to preserve for a while their once terrible names." Now the plan laid down by the president, in order to prevent, if possible, the total decay of the Indian people, is, to send them beyond the Mississippi, and *guarantee* to them the possession of ample territory west of that river. How far this is likely to answer the purpose *expressed*, let us now examine.

The Cherokees, by their intercourse with and proximity to the white people, have become half civilized; and how is it likely that *their* condition will be improved by driving them into the forests and barren prairies? That territory is at present the haunt of the Pawnees, the Osages, and other warlike nations, who live almost entirely by the chase, and are constantly waging war even with each other. As soon as the Cherokees, and other half-civilized Indians, appear, they will be regarded as common intruders, and be subject to the united attacks of these people. There are even old feuds existing among themselves, which, it is but too probable, may be renewed. Trappers and hunters, in large parties, yearly make incursions into the country beyond the boundaries of the United States, and in defiance of the Indians kill the beaver and the buffalo—the latter merely for the *tongue and skin*, leaving the carcase to rot upon the ground.[16] Thus is this unfortunate race robbed of their means of subsistence. Moreover, what guarantee can the Indians have, that the United States will keep faith for the future, when it is admitted that they have not done so in times past? How can they be sure that they may not further be driven from river to river, and from mountain to mountain, until they reach the shores of the Pacific; and who can tell but that then it may be found expedient to drive them into the ocean?

The policy of the United States government is evidently to get the Indians to exterminate each other. Its whole proceedings from the time this question was first agitated to the present, but too clearly indicate this intention; and if we wanted proof, that the executive government of the United States *would act* on so barbarous and inhuman a policy, we need only refer to the allocation of the Cherokees, who exchanged lands in Tennessee for lands west of the Mississippi, pursuant to the treaty of 1819. It was well known that a deadly enmity existed between the Osages and Cherokees, and that any proximity of the two people, would inevitably lead to fatal results; yet, with this knowledge, the executive government placed those Cherokees in the country lying between the Arkansaw and Red rivers, *immediately joining the territory of the Osages.* It is unnecessary to state that the result was *as anticipated*—they daily committed outrages upon the persons and properties of each other, and the death of many warriors, on both sides, ensued.

The sympathy expressed in that part of the Message relating to the Indians, if expressed with sincerity, would do much honour to the feelings that dictated it; but when we come to examine the facts, and investigate the implied allegations, we shall find that they are most gratuitous; and, consequently, that the regret of the president at the probable fate of the Indian, should he remain east of the Mississippi, is grossly hypocritical. He says, "surrounded by the whites, with their arts of civilization, which, by destroying the resources of the savage, doom him to weakness and decay:[17] the fate of the Mohegan, the Narragansett, and the Delaware, is fast overtaking the Choctaw, the Cherokee, and the Creek. That this fate surely awaits them, if they remain within the limits of the States, does not admit of a doubt. Humanity and national honour demand that every effort should be made to avert so great a calamity." From what facts the president has drawn these conclusions does not appear. Neither the statements of the Cherokees, nor of the Indian agents, nor the report of the secretary of war, furnish any such information; on the contrary, with the exception of one or two agents *at Washington*, all give the most flattering accounts of advancement in civilization. The Rev. Samuel A. Worcester, in his letter to the Rev. E.S. Ely, editor of the "Philadelphian," completely refutes all the unfavourable statements that have been got up to cover the base conduct of Jackson and the slavites. This gentleman has resided for the last four years among the Cherokees, and has surely had abundant means of observing their condition.

The letter of David Brown (a Cherokee), addressed, September 2, 1825, to the editor of "The Family Visitor," at Richmond, Virginia, states, that "the Cherokee plains are covered with herds of cattle—sheep, goats, and swine, cover the valleys and hills—the plains and valleys are rich, and produce Indian corn, cotton, tobacco, wheat, oats, indigo, sweet and Irish potatoes, &c. The natives carry on a considerable trade with the adjoining states, and some of them export cotton in boats down the Tennessee to the Mississippi, and down that river to New Orleans. Orchards are common—cheese, butter, &c. plenty—houses of entertainment are kept by natives. Cotton and woollen cloths are manufactured in the nation, and almost every family grows cotton for its own consumption. Agricultural pursuits engage the chief attention of the nation—different branches of mechanics are pursued. Schools are increasing every year, and education is encouraged and rewarded." To quote David Brown verbatim, on the population,—"In the year 1819, an estimate was made of the Cherokees. Those on the west were estimated at 5,000, and those on the east of the Mississippi, at 10,000 souls. The census of this division of the Cherokees has again been taken within the current year (1825), and the returns are thus made: native citizens, 13,563; white men married in the nation, 147; white women ditto, 73; African slaves, 1177. If this summary of the Cherokee population, from the census, is correct, to say nothing of those of foreign extract, we find that in six years the increase has been 3,563 souls. National pride, patriotism, and a spirit of independence, mark the Cherokee character." He further states, "the system of government is founded on republican principles, and secures the respect of the people." An alphabet has been invented by an Indian, named George Guess, the Cherokee Cadmus, and a printing press has been established at New Echota, the seat of government, where there is published weekly a paper entitled, "The Cherokee Phoenix,"—one half being in the English language, and the other in that of the Cherokee.

The report of the secretary of war, upon the present condition of the Indians, states of the Chickesaws and Choctaws, all that has been above said of the Cherokees. But of the last-mentioned people, the secretary's accounts appear to be studiously defective. Yet the fact is notorious, that both the Chickesaws and Choctaws are far behind the Cherokees in civilization.

With these facts before our eyes, what are we to think of the grief of the president, at the decay and increasing weakness of the Cherokees? Can it be regarded in any way but as a piece of shameless hypocrisy, too glaring in its character to escape the notice even of the most inobservant individual. It has been said that the question involves many difficulties—to me there appears none. The United States, in the year 1791, guarantee to the Indians the possession of all their lands not then ceded—and confirm this by numerous subsequent treaties. In 1802, they promise to Georgia, the possession of the Cherokee lands "*whenever such purchase could be made on reasonable terms*" This is the simple state of the case; and if the executive were inclined to act uprightly, the line of conduct to be pursued could be determined on without much difficulty. Georgia has no right to press upon the executive the fulfilment of engagements which were made conditionally, and consequently with an implied reservation; and the United States should not violate *many positive treaties*, in order to fulfil *a conditional one*.[18]

I shall now advert to some of the charges touching the character of the Indians. It is said, that they are debauched and insincere. This charge has been particularly made against the Creeks, and I believe is not altogether unfounded. Yet, if this be now the character of the once warlike and noble Creek, let the white man ask himself who has made him so? Who makes the "firewater," and who supplies the untutored savage with the means of intoxication? The white-man, when he wishes to trade profitably with the

Indian, fills the cup, and holds it forth—he says, 'drink, my brother, it is good'—the red-man drinks, and the wily white points at his condition, says he is uncivilized, and should go forth from the land, for his presence is contamination!

As to the charge of hypocrisy—this too has been taught or forced upon the Indians by the conduct of the whites. Missionaries have been constantly going among them, teaching dogmas and doctrines, far beyond the comprehension of some learned white-men, and to the savage totally unintelligible. These gentlemen have told long stories; and when posed by some quaint saying, or answered by some piece of traditional information, handed down from generation to generation, by the fathers and mothers of the tribe, have found it necessary to purchase the acquiescence of a few Indians by bribes, in order that their labours might not seem to have been altogether unsuccessful. This conduct of the Missionaries was soon *understood* by the Indians, and the temptation held out was too great to be resisted. Blankets and gowns converted, when inspiration and gospel truths had failed.

Mr. Houston of Tennessee, after having attained the honour of being governor of his state, and having enjoyed all the consideration necessarily attached to that office, at length became tired of civilized life, and retired among the Creeks to end his days. He has resided long among them, and knows their character well; yet, in one of his statements made to the Indian board at New York, he says, that the attempts to Christianize the Indians in their present state, he was of opinion, much as he honoured the zeal that had prompted them, were fruitless, *or worse.* The supposed conversions had produced no change of habits. So degraded had become the character of this once independent people, that professions of religious belief had been made, and the ordinances of religion submitted to, "when an Indian wanted a new blanket, or a squaw a new gown."[19] Thus, according to governor Houston, the only fruits produced by the boasted labours of the missionaries, have been dissimulation and deceit; and demoralization has been the result of teaching *doctrinal* Christianity to the children of the forest. Yet we must, in candour, acknowledge that Mr. Houston is not singular in that opinion, since we find, so far back as the year 1755, Cadwallader Calden express himself much to the same effect. "The Five Nations," he says, "are a poor and generally called barbarous people, bred under the darkest ignorance; and yet a bright and noble genius shines through these black clouds. None of the greatest Roman heroes have discovered a greater love of country, or contempt of death, than these people, called barbarous, have shown when liberty came in competition. Indeed I think our Indians have outdone the Romans in this particular. Some of the greatest of those Roman heroes have murdered themselves to avoid shame or torments; but our Indians have refused to die meanly or with little pain, when they thought their country's honour would be at stake by it; but have given their bodies willingly to the most cruel torments of their enemies, to show, as they said, that 'the Five Nations' consisted of men whose courage and resolution could not be shaken. But what, alas! have we Christians done to make them better? We have, indeed, reason to be ashamed that these infidels, by our conversation and neighbourhood, are become worse than they were before they knew us. Instead of virtue, we have only taught them vice, that they were entirely free from before that time."[20] The Rev. Timothy Flint, who was himself a missionary, in his "Ten Years' Residence in the Valley of the Mississippi," observes, page 144,—"I have surely had it in my heart to impress them with the importance of the subject (religion). I have scarcely noticed an instance in which the subject was not received either with indifference, rudeness, or jesting. Of all races of men that I have seen, they seem most incapable of religious impressions. They have, indeed, some notions of an invisible agent, but they seemed generally to think that the Indians had their god as the whites had theirs." And again, "nothing will eventually be gained to the great cause by colouring and mis-statement," alluding to the practice of the missionaries; "and however reluctant we may be to receive it, the real state of things will eventually be known to us. We have heard of the imperishable labours of an Elliott and a Brainard, in other days. But in these times it is a melancholy truth, that Protestant exertions to Christianize them have not been marked with apparent success. The Catholics have caused many to hang a crucifix around their necks, which they show as they show their medals and other ornaments, and this is too often all they have to mark them as Christians. We have read the narratives of the Catholics, which detailed the most glowing and animating views of success. I have had accounts, however, from travellers in these regions, that have been over the Stony mountains into the great missionary settlements of St. Peter and St. Paul. These travellers (and some of them were professed Catholics) unite in affirming that the converts will escape from the missions whenever it is in their power, fly into their native deserts, and resume at once their old mode of life."

That the vast sums expended on missions should have produced so little effect, we may consider lamentable, but it is lamentably true; for in addition to the mass of evidence we have to that effect, from disinterested white men, we have also the speeches and communications of the Indians themselves. The celebrated Seneca chief, Saguyuwhaha (keeper awake), better known in the United States by the name of Red-jacket, in a letter communicated to Governor De Witt Clinton, at a treaty held at Albany, says, "Our great father, the President, has recommended to our young men to be industrious, to plough and to sow. This we have done; and we are thankful for the advice, and for the means he has afforded us of carrying it into effect. We are happier in consequence of it; *but another thing recommended to us, has created great confusion among us, and is making us a quarrelsome and divided people; and that is, the introduction of preachers into our nation.* These black-coats contrive to get the consent of some of the Indians to preach among us; and whenever this is the case, confusion and disorder are sure to follow, and the encroachment of the whites on our lands is the inevitable consequence.

"The governor must not think hard of me for speaking thus of the preachers: I have observed their progress, and whenever I look back to see what has taken place of old, I perceive that whenever they came among the Indians, they were the forerunners of their dispersion; that they always excited enmities and quarrels amongst them; that they introduced the white people on their lands, by whom they were robbed and plundered of their property; and that the Indians were sure to dwindle and decrease, and be driven back, in proportion to the number of preachers that came among them.

"Each nation has its own customs and its own religion. The Indians have theirs, given them by the Great Spirit, under which they were happy. It was not intended that they should embrace the religion of the whites, and be destroyed by the attempt to make them think differently on that subject from their fathers.

"It is true, these preachers have got the consent of some of the chiefs to stay and preach amongst us; but I and my friends know this to be wrong, and that they ought to be removed; besides, we have been threatened by Mr. Hyde—who came among us as a schoolmaster and a teacher of our children, but has now become a black-coat, and refuses to teach them any more—that unless we listen to his preaching and become Christians, we shall be turned off our lands. We wish to know from the governor, if this is to be so? and if he has no right to say so, we think *he* ought to be turned off our lands, and not allowed to plague us any more. We shall never be at peace while he is among us.

"We are afraid too, that these preachers, by and by, will become poor, *and force us to pay them for living among us, and disturbing us.*

"Some of our chiefs have got lazy, and instead of cultivating their lands themselves, employ white people to do so. There are now eleven families living on our reservation at Buffalo; this is wrong, and ought not to be permitted. The great source of all our grievances is, that the whites are among us. Let *them* be removed, and we will be happy and contented among ourselves. We now cry to the governor for help, and hope that he will attend to our complaints, and speedily give us redress."[21]

This melancholy hostility to the missionaries is not confined to a particular tribe or nation of Indians, for all those people, in every situation, from the base of the Alleghanies to the foot of the Rocky mountains, declare the same sentiments on this subject; and although policy or courtesy may induce some chiefs to express themselves less strongly than Red-jacket has expressed himself, we have but too many proofs that their feelings are not more moderate. On the fourth of February, 1822, the president of the United States, in council, received a deputation of Indians, from the principal nations west of the Mississippi, who came under the protection of Major O'Fallon, when each chief delivered a speech on the occasion. I shall here insert an extract from that of the "Wandering Pawnee" chief, more as a specimen of Indian wisdom and eloquence than as bearing particularly on the subject. Speaking of the Great Spirit, he said, "We worship him not as you do. We differ from you in appearance, and manners, as well as in our customs; and we differ from you in our religion. We have no large houses, as you have, to worship the Great Spirit in: if we had them to-day, we should want others to-morrow; for we have not like you a fixed habitation—we have no settled home except our villages, where we remain but two months in twelve. We, like animals, rove through the country; whilst you whites reside between us and heaven. But still, my great Father, we love the Great Spirit—we acknowledge his supreme power—our peace, our health, and our happiness depend upon him, and our lives belong to him—he made us, and he can destroy us.

"My great Father,—some of your good chiefs, as they are called (missionaries), have proposed to send some of their good people among us to change our habits, to make us work for them, and live like the white people. I will not tell a lie—I am going to tell the truth. You love your country—you love your people—you love the manner in which they live, and you think your people brave. I am like you, my great Father; I love my country—I love my people—I love the manner in which we live, and think myself and warriors brave.[22] Spare me then, my Father; let me enjoy my country, and pursue the buffalo and the beaver, and the other wild animals of our country, and I will trade their skins with your people. I have grown up and lived thus long without work—I am in hopes you will suffer me to die without it. We have plenty of buffalo, beaver, deer, and other wild animals—we have also an abundance of horses—we have every thing we want—we have plenty of land, *if you will keep your people off it.* My Father has a piece on which he lives (Council bluffs), and we wish him to enjoy it—we have enough without it—but we wish him to live near us, to give us good council—to keep our ears and eyes open, that we may continue to pursue the right road—the road to happiness. He settles all differences between us and the whites, between the red-skins themselves—he makes the whites do justice to the red-skins, and he makes the red-skins do justice to the whites. He saves the effusion of human blood, and restores peace and happiness in the land. You have already sent us a father (Major O'Fallon); it is enough—he knows us, and we know him—we keep our eye constantly upon him, and since we have heard *your* words, we will listen more attentively to *his*.

"It is too soon, my great Father, to send those good chiefs amongst us. *We are not starving yet*—we wish you to permit us to enjoy the chase until the game of our country is exhausted—until the wild animals become extinct. Let us exhaust our present resources before you make us toil and interrupt our happiness. Let me continue to live as I have done; and after I have passed to the good or evil spirit, from off the wilderness of my present life, the subsistence of my children may become so precarious as to need and embrace the assistance of those good people.

"There was a time when we did not know the whites—our wants were then fewer than they are now. They were always within our control—we had then seen nothing which we could not get. Before our intercourse with the whites (who have caused such a destruction in our game) we could lie down to sleep, and when we awoke we would find the buffalo feeding around our camp—but now we are killing them for their skins, and feeding the wolves with their flesh, to make our children cry over their bones.

"Here, my great Father, is a pipe which I present to you, as I am accustomed to present pipes to all the Red-skins in peace with us. It is filled with such tobacco as we were accustomed to smoke before we knew the white people. It is pleasant, and the spontaneous growth of the most remote parts of our country. I know that the robes, leggings, and moccasins, and bear-claws are of little value to *you*; but we wish you to have them deposited and preserved in some conspicuous part of your lodge, so that when we are gone and the sod turned over our bones, if our children should visit this place, as we do now, they may see and recognize with pleasure the depositories of their fathers; and reflect on the times that are past."

I shall now take leave of the Indians and their political condition, by observing that the proceedings of the American government, throughout, towards this brave but unfortunate race, have only been exceeded in atrocity by the past and present conduct of the East India government towards the pusillanimous but unoffending Hindoos.

Note.—This chapter I wrote during my stay in Kentucky, and the first part of it, in substance, was inserted in the "Kentucky Intelligencer," at the request of the talented editor and proprietor, John Mullay, Esq.

FOOTNOTES:

[15]

In November, 1785, during the articles of confederation, a treaty is concluded with the Cherokees, which establishes a boundary, and allots to the Indians a great extent of country, now within the limits of North Carolina and Georgia.

In 1791, the treaty of Holston is concluded; by which a new boundary is agreed upon. This was the first treaty made by the United States under their present constitution; and by the seventh article, a solemn guarantee is given for all the lands not then ceded.

On the 7th of February, 1792, by an additional article to the last treaty, 500 dollars are added to the stipulated annuity.

In June, 1794, another treaty is entered into, in which the provisions of the treaty of 1791 are revived, an addition is made to the annuity, and provision made for marking the boundary line.

In October, 1798, a treaty is concluded which revives former treaties, and curtails the boundary of Indian lands by a cession to the United States, for an additional compensation.

In October, 1804, a treaty is concluded, by which, for a consideration specified, more land is ceded.

In October, 1805, two treaties are made, by which an additional quantity of land is ceded.

On 7th January, 1806, by another treaty, more land is ceded to the United States.

In September, 1807, the boundary line intended in the last treaty, is satisfactorily ascertained.

On 22d March, 1816, a treaty is concluded, by which lands in South Carolina are ceded, for which the United States engage South Carolina shall pay. On the same day another treaty is made, by which the Indians agree to allow the use of the water-courses in their country, and also to permit roads to be made through the same.

On the 14th of September, 1816, a treaty is made, by which an additional quantity of land is ceded to the United States.

On the 8th of July, 1817, a treaty is concluded, by which an exchange of lands is agreed on, and a plan for dividing the Cherokees settled.

On the 27th of February, 1819, another treaty is concluded, in execution of the stipulations contained in that of 1817, in several particulars, and in which an additional tract of country is ceded to the United States.

[16]

"The white hunter, on encamping in his journeys, cuts down green trees, and builds a large fire of long logs, sitting at some distance from it. The Indian hunts up a few dry limbs, cracks them into little pieces a foot in length, builds a small fire, and sits close to it. He gets as much warmth as the white hunter without half the labour, and does not burn more than a fiftieth part of the wood. The Indian considers the forest his own, and is careful in using and preserving every thing which it affords. He never kills more than he has occasion for. The white hunter destroys all before him, and cannot resist the opportunity of killing game, although he neither wants the meat nor can carry the skins. I was particularly struck with this wanton practice, which lately occurred on White river. A hunter returning from the woods, heavily laden with the flesh and skins of five bears, unexpectedly arrived in the midst of a drove of buffalos, and wantonly shot down three, having no other object than the sport of killing them. This is one of the causes of the enmity existing between the white and red hunters of Missouri".—*Schoolcroft's Tour in Missouri*, page 52.

[17]

Does the General include among the arts of civilization, that of systematically robbing the Indians of their farms and hunting grounds? If so, no doubt *these arts of civilization*, must inevitably "destroy the resources of the savage," and "doom him to weakness and decay."

[18]

The Indians apply the term "Christian honesty," precisely in the same sense that the Romans applied "*Punica fides*."

[19]

There is an old Indian at present in the Missouri territory, to whom his tribe has given the cognomen of "much-water," from the circumstance of his having been baptized so frequently.

[20]

Heriot says (page 320), "They have evinced a decided attachment to their ancient habits, and have *gained* less from the means that might have smoothed the asperities of their condition, than they have *lost* by copying the vices of those, who exhibited to their view the arts of civilization."

[21]

This letter was dictated by Red-jacket, and interpreted by Henry Obeal, in the presence of ten chiefs, whose names are affixed, at Canandaigua, January 18, 1821.

[22]

"The attachment which savages entertain for their mode of life supersedes every allurement, however powerful, to change it. Many Frenchmen have lived with them, and have imbibed such an invincible partiality for that independent and erratic condition, that no means could prevail on them to abandon it. On the contrary, no single instance has yet occurred of a savage being able to reconcile himself to a state of civilization. Infants have been taken from among the natives, and educated with much care in France, where they could not possibly have intercourse with their countrymen and relations. Although they had remained several years in that country, and could not form the smallest idea of the wilds of America, the force of blood predominated over that of education: no sooner did they find themselves at liberty than they tore their clothes in pieces, and went to traverse the forests in search of their countrymen, whose mode of life appeared to them far more agreeable than that which they had led among the French."—*Heriot*, p. 354.

This passage of Heriot's is taken nearly verbatim from Charlevoix, v. 2, p. 109.

CHAPTER X

I left Kentucky, and passed up the river to Wheeling, in Virginia. There is little worthy of observation encountered in a passage up this part of the Ohio, except the peculiar character of the stream, which has been before alluded to. At Marietta, at the mouth of the Muskingum, ship-building is carried on; and vessels have been constructed at Pittsburg, full 2000 miles from the gulf of Mexico. About seventy miles up the Kenhawa river, in Virginia, are situated the celebrated salt springs, the most productive of any in the Union. They are at present in the possession of a chartered company, which limits the manufacture to 800,000 bushels annually, but it is estimated that the fifty-seven wells are capable of yielding 50,000 bushels each, per annum, which would make an aggregate of 2,850,000 bushels. Many of these springs issue out of rocks, and the water is so strongly impregnated with salt, that from 90 to 130 gallons yield a bushel. The whole western country bordering the Ohio and its tributaries, is supplied with salt from these works.

Wheeling, although not large, enjoys a considerable share of commercial intercourse, being an entrepôt for eastern merchandize, which is transported from the Atlantic cities across the mountains to this town and Pittsburg, and from thence by water to the different towns along the rivers.

The process of "hauling" merchandize from Baltimore and Philadelphia to the banks of the Ohio, and *vice versâ*, is rather tedious, the roads lying across steep and rugged mountains. Large covered waggons, light and strong, drawn by five or six horses, two and two, are employed for this purpose. The waggoner always rides the near shaft horse, and guides the team by means of reins, a whip, and his voice. The time generally consumed in one of these journeys is from twenty to twenty-five days.

All the mountains or hills on the upper part of the Ohio, from Wheeling to Pittsburg, contain immense beds of coal; this added to the mineral productions, particularly that of iron ore, which abound in this section of country, offers advantages for manufacturing, which are of considerable importance, and are fully appreciated. Pittsburg is called the Birmingham of America. Some of those coal beds are well circumstanced, the coal being found immediately under the super-stratum, and the galleries frequently running out on the high road. Notwithstanding the local advantages, and the protection and encouragement at present afforded by the tariff, England need never fear any extensive competition with her manufactures in foreign markets from America, as the high spirit of the people of that country will always prevent them from pursuing, extensively, the sordid occupations of the loom or the workshop.

The upper parts of Virginia and Pennsylvania are in a high state of improvement; the land is hilly, and the face of the country picturesque. The farms are well cultivated, and there is a large portion of pasture land in this and the adjoining states. I encountered several large droves of horses and black cattle on their way to the neighbourhood of Philadelphia and to the state of New York. The black cattle are purchased principally in Ohio, whence they are brought into the Atlantic states, to be fattened and consumed. The farmers and their families in Pennsylvania, have an appearance of comfort and respectability a good deal resembling that of the substantial English yeoman; yet farming here, as in all parts of the country, is a laborious occupation.

I crossed the Monongahela at Williamsport, and the Youghaghany at Robstown, and so on through Mountpleasant to the first ridge of mountains, called "the chestnut ridge." I determined on crossing the mountains on foot; and after having made arrangements to that effect, I commenced sauntering along the road. Near Mountpleasant, I stopped to dine at the house of a Dutchman by descent. After dinner, the party adjourned, as is customary, to the bar-room, when divers political and polemical topics were canvassed with the usual national warmth. An account of his late Majesty's death was inserted in a Philadelphia paper, and happened to be noticed by one of the politicians present, when the landlord asked me how we elected our king in England. I replied that he was not elected, but that he became king by birthright, &c. A Kentuckian observed, placing his leg on the back of the next chair, "That's a kind of unnatural." An Indianian said, "I don't believe in that system myself." A third—"Do you mean to tell me, that because the last king was a smart man and knew his duty, that his son, or his brother, should be a smart man, and fit for the situation?" I explained that we had a premier, ministers, &c.;—when the last gentleman replied, "Then you pay half-a-dozen men to do one man's business. Yes—yes—that may do for Englishmen very well; but, I guess, it would not go down here—no, no, Americans are a little more enlightened than to stand that kind of wiggery." During this conversation, a person had stepped into the room, and had taken his seat in silence. I was about to reply to the last observations of my antagonist, when this gentleman opened out, with, "yes! that may do for Englishmen very well"—he was an Englishman, I knew at once by his accent, and I verily believe the identical radical who set the village of Bracebridge by the ears, and pitched the villagers to the devil, on seeing them grin through a horse-collar, when they should have been calculating the interest of the national debt, or conning over the list of sinecure placemen. He held in his hand, instead of "Cobbett's Register," the "Greenville Republican."—He had substituted for his short-sleeved coat, "a round-about."—He seemed to have put on flesh, and looked somewhat more contented. "Yes, yes," he says, "that may do for Englishmen very well, but it won't do here. Here we make our own laws, and we keep them too. It may do for Englishmen very well, to have *the liberty* of paying taxes for the support of the nobility. To have *the liberty* of being incarcerated in a gaol, for shooting the wild animals of the country. To have *the liberty* of being seized by a press-gang, torn away from their wives and families, and flogged at the discretion of my lord Tom, Dick, or Harry's bastard." At this, the Kentuckian gnashed his teeth, and instinctively grasped his hunting-knife;—an old Indian doctor, who was squatting in one corner of the room, said, slowly and emphatically, as his eyes glared, his nostrils dilated, and his lip curled with contempt—"The Englishman is a dog"—while a Georgian slave, who stood behind his master's chair, grinned and chuckled with delight, as he said—"*poor* Englishman, him meaner man den black nigger."—"To have," continued the Englishman, "*the liberty* of being transported for seven years for being caught learning the use of the sword or the musket. To have the tenth lamb, and the tenth sheaf seized, or the blanket torn from off his bed, to pay a bloated, a plethoric bishop or parson,—to be kicked and cuffed about by a parcel of 'Bourbon *gendarmerie*'—Liberty!—why hell sweat"—here I—slipped out at the side door into the water-melon patch. As I receded, I heard the whole party burst out into an obstreperous fit of laughter.—A few broken sentences, from the Kentuckian and the radical, reached my ear, such as "backed out"—"damned aristocratic." I returned in about half an hour to pay my bill, when I could observe one or two of those doughty politicians who remained, leering at me most significantly. However, I—"smiled, and said nothing."

"The Chestnut ridge" is a chain of rocky, barren mountains, covered with wood, and the ascent is steep and difficult. It is named from the quantity of chestnut trees that compose the bulk of its timber. Being a little fatigued in ascending, I sat down in a wood of scrub oak. When I had been some time seated on a large stone, my ear caught the gliding of a snake. Turning quickly, I perceived, at about a yard's distance, a reptile of that beautiful species the rattle-snake. He ceased moving: I jumped up, and struck at his head with a stick, but missed the blow. He instantly coiled and rattled. I now retreated beyond the range of his spring. Perceiving that I had no intention of giving him fair play by coming within his reach, he suddenly uncoiled and glid across a log, thinking to make good his retreat; but being determined on having—not his scalp, for the head of a rattle-snake is rather a dangerous toy—but his rattle, I pursued him across the log. He now coiled again, and rattled most furiously, thus indicating his extreme wrath at being attacked: the bite of this reptile is most venomous when he is most enraged. I took up a flat stone, about six inches square, and lobbed it on his coil. He suddenly darted out towards me; but, as I had anticipated, he was encumbered with the stone. I now advanced, and struck him on the head with my stick. I repeated the blow until he seemed to be deprived of sensation, when I drew my hunting knife and decapitated him. For a full hour afterwards the body retained all the vigour and sensitiveness which it possessed previous to decapitation, and on touching any part of it, would twist round in the same manner as when the animal was perfect. Sensation gradually disappeared, departing first from the extremities—more towards the wounded extremity than towards the other, but gradually from both, until it was entirely gone. The length of this reptile was about four feet, and the skin was extremely beautiful. Nothing could exceed the beauty of his eye. A clear black lustre characterizes the eye of this animal, and is said to produce so powerful an effect on birds and smaller animals, as to deprive them of the power of escaping. This snake had eight rattles, so that he must have been at least eleven years old. I understood afterwards that there was a rattle-snakes' den in the neighbourhood. They appear to live in society, and the large quantities that are frequently found congregated together are astonishing. The Jacksonville (Illinois) Gazette of the 22d April, 1830, says, "Last week, a den of rattle-snakes was discovered near Apple Creek, by a person while engaged in digging for rock in that part of our country. He made known the circumstance to the neighbours, who visited the place, where they killed 193 rattle-snakes, the largest of which (as our informant, who was on the spot, told us) measured nearly four feet in length. Besides these, there were sixteen black snakes destroyed, together with one copper-head. Counting the young ones, there were upwards of 1000 killed." There are two species of rattle-snake, which are in constant hostility with each other. The common black snake, whose bite is perfectly innoxious, and the copper-head, have also a deadly enmity towards the rattle-snake, which, when they meet it, they never fail to attack.

The next ridge of mountains is called the "laurel hills," which are covered with an immense growth of different species of laurel. Between these and the Alleghany ridge are situated "the glades"—beautiful fertile plains in a high state of cultivation. This district is most healthy, and fevers and agues are unknown to the inhabitants. Here the "Delawares of the hills" once roamed the sole lords of this fine country; and perhaps from the very eminence from whence I contemplated the beauty of the scene, some warrior, returning from the "war path" or the chase, may have gazed with pleasure on the hills of his fathers, the possessions of a long line of Sylvan heros, and in the pride of manhood said—'The Delawares are men—they are strong in battle, and cunning on the trail of their foes—at the 'council fire' there is wisdom in their words. Who counts more scalps than the Lenni Lenapé warrior?—he can never be conquered—the stranger shall never dwell in his glades.' Where now is the "Delaware of the hills?"—gone!—his very name is unknown in his own land, and not a vestige remains to tell that *there* once dwelt a great and powerful tribe. When the white man falls, his high towers and lofty battlements are laid crumbling with the dust, yet these mighty ruins remain for ages, monuments of his former greatness: but the Indian passes away, silent as the noiseless tread of the moccasin—the next snow comes, and his "trail" is blotted out for ever.

I toiled across the Alleghanies, which are completely covered with timber, and passed on to a place within about thirty miles of Chambersburg, on a branch of the Potomac. Here, coming in upon *civilization*, I took the stage to Baltimore. In my pedestrian excursion the road lay for several miles along the banks of the Juniata, which is a very fine river. The scenery is romantic, and is much beautified by a large growth of magnificent pines. The Alleghany ridge is composed chiefly of sand-stone, clay-slate, and lime-stone-slate, sand-stone sometimes in large blocks.

I encountered several parties of French, Irish, Swiss, Bavarians, Dutch, &c. going westward, with swarms of children, and considerable quantities of household lumber:—symptoms of seeking *El dorado*.

In the neighbourhood of Baltimore there are many handsome residences, and the farms are all well cleared, and in many cases walled in. The number of comparatively miserable-looking cabins which are dispersed along the road near this town, and the long lists of crimes and misdemeanours with which the Journals of Baltimore and Philadelphia are filled, sufficiently indicate that these cities have arrived to an advanced state of civilization. For, wherever there are very rich people, there must be very poor people; and wherever there are very poor people, there must necessarily exist a proportionate quantity of crime. Men are poor, only because they are ignorant; for if they possessed a knowledge of their own powers and capabilities, they would then know, that however wealth may be distributed, all real wealth is created by labour, and by labour alone.

Baltimore is seated on the north side of the Patapsco river, within a few miles of the Chesapeak bay. It received its name in compliment to the Irish family of the Calverts. The harbour, at Fell Point, has about eighteen feet water, and is defended by a strong fort, called Mc Henry's fort, on Observation Hill. Vessels of large tonnage cannot enter the basin. In 1791 it contained 13,503 inhabitants; in 1810, 46,487; and at present it contains 80,519. There are many fine buildings and monuments in this city; and the streets in which business is not extensively transacted, are planted with Lombardy poplar, locust, and pride-of-china trees,—the last mentioned especially afford a fine shade.

A considerable schooner trade is carried on by the merchants of Baltimore with South America. The schooners of this port are celebrated for their beauty, and are much superior to those of any other port on the Continent. They are sharp built, somewhat resembling the small Greek craft one sees in the Mediterranean. A rail-road is being constructed from this place to the Ohio river, a distance of upwards of three hundred miles, and about fourteen miles of the road is already completed, as is also a viaduct. If the enterprising inhabitants of Baltimore be able to finish this undertaking, it must necessarily throw a very large amount of wealth into their hands, to the prejudice of Philadelphia and New York. But the expense will be enormous.

I left Baltimore for Philadelphia in one of those splendid and spacious steam-boats peculiar to this country. We paddled up the Chesapeak bay until we came to Elk river—the scenery at both sides is charming. A little distance up this river commences the "Chesapeak and Delaware canal," which passes through the old state of Delaware, and unites the waters of the two bays. Here we were handed into a barge, or what we in common parlance would term a large canal boat; but the Americans are the fondest people in the universe of big names, and ransack the Dictionary for the most pompous appellations with which to designate their works or productions. The universal fondness for European titles that obtains here, is also remarkable. The president, is "his excellency,"—"congressmen," are "honorables,"—and every petty merchant, or "dry-goods store-keeper," is, at least, an esquire. Their newspapers contain many specimens of this love of monarchical distinctions—such as, "wants a situation, as store-keeper (shopman), a gentleman, &c." "Two gentlemen were convicted and sentenced to six months' imprisonment for horse-stealing, &c." These two items I read myself in the papers of the western country, and the latter was commented on by a Philadelphia journal. You may frequently see "Miss Amanda," without shoes or stockings—certainly for convenience or economy, not from necessity, and generally in Dutch houses—and "that *ere* young lady" scouring the pails! An accident lately occurred in one of the factories in New England, and the local paper stated, that "one young lady was seriously injured,"—this young lady was a spinner. Observe, I by no means object to the indiscriminate use of the terms *gentleman* and *lady*, but merely state the fact. On the contrary, so far am I from finding fault with the practice, that I think it quite fair; when any portion of republicans make use of terms which properly belong to a monarchy, that all classes should do the same, it being unquestionably their right. It does not follow, because a man may be introduced as an *American gentleman*, that he may not be simply a mechanic.

The Chesapeak and Delaware canal is about fourteen miles in length; and from the nature of the soil through which it is cut, there was some difficulty attending the permanent security of the work. On reaching the Delaware, we were again handed into a steamer, and so conducted to Philadelphia. The merchant shipping, and the numerous pleasure and steam-boats, and craft of every variety, which are constantly moving on the broad bosom of the Delaware, present a gay and animated scene.

Philadelphia is a regular well-built city, and one of the handsomest in the states. It lies in latitude 39° 56' north, and longitude, west of London, 75° 8'; distant from the sea, 120 miles. The city stands on an elevated piece of ground between the Schuylkill and Delaware rivers, about a mile broad from bank to bank, and six miles from their junction. The Delaware is about a mile wide at Philadelphia, and ships of the largest tonnage can approach the wharf. The city contains many fine buildings of Schuylkill marble. The streets are well paved, and have broad *trottoirs* of hard red brick. The police regulations are excellent, and cleanliness is much attended to, the kennels being washed daily during the summer months, with water from the reservoirs. The markets, or shambles, extend half-a-mile in length, from the wharf up Market-street, in six divisions. In addition to the shambles, farmers' waggons, loaded with every kind of country produce for sale, line the street.

There are five banking establishments in the city: the Bank of North America, the United States Bank, the Bank of Pennsylvania, the Bank of Philadelphia, and the Farmers' Bank.

The principal institutions are, the Franklin library, which contains upwards of 20,000 volumes. Strangers are admitted gratis, and are permitted to peruse any of the books. The Americans should adopt this practice in all their national exhibitions, and rather copy the liberality of the French than the sordid churlishness of the English, who compel foreigners to pay even for seeing the property of the nation. The other institutions are, the University of Pennsylvania, a College, Medical Theatre, College of Physicians, Philosophical Hall, Agricultural and Linnean Societies, Academy of Fine Arts, and the Cincinnati Society, which originated in an attempt to establish a sort of aristocracy. The members were at its formation the surviving officers of the revolution; they wear an eagle, suspended by a ribbon, which, at their death, they have appointed to be taken by their eldest sons. There are besides, the Academies of the Philadelphian Friends, and the German Lutherans; Sunday and Lancasterian schools; and, of course, divers Bible and Tract Societies, which are patronized by all the antiquated dames in the city, and superintended by the Methodist and Presbyterian parsons. The Methodist parsons of this country have the character of being men of gallantry; and indeed, from the many instances I have heard of their propensity in this way, from young Americans, I should be a very sceptic to doubt the fact.

There are also St. George's, St. Patrick's, St. David's, and St. Andrew's Societies for the relief and colonization of British emigrants; a French and a German Emigrant Society, and several hospitals. There are two theatres and an amphitheatre. Peal's Museum contains a large collection, which is scientifically arranged; among other fossils is the perfect skeleton of a mammoth, found in a bed of marle in the state of New York. The length of this animal, from the bend of the tusks to the rump, was about twenty-seven feet, and the height and bulk proportionate.

The navy-yard contains large quantities of timber, spars, and rigging, prepared for immediate use, as also warlike stores of every description. There is here, a ship of 140 guns, of large calibre, and a frigate. Both are housed completely, and in a condition to be launched in a few months, if necessary. They are constructed of the very best materials, and in the most durable and solid manner. There are now being constructed, seriatim, twenty-five ships of the line—one for every state in the Union. The government occasionally sells the smaller vessels of war to merchants, in order to increase the shipping, and to secure that those armed vessels which are afloat, may be in the finest possible condition. A corvette, completely equipped, was lately sold to his majesty the autocrat of the Russias; but was dismasted in a day or two after her departure from Charleston. She was taken in tow by the vessel of a New York merchant, and carried into the port of that city. The merchant refused any compensation from the Russian minister, although his vessel was, when she fell in with the wreck, proceeding to the Austral regions, and her putting about was greatly disadvantageous. The minister returned thanks publicly, on the part of his master, and expressed his majesty's sense of the invariable consideration and friendship with which his majesty's subjects are treated by the citizens of America. There appears to be a universal wish among the Americans to cultivate an alliance, offensive and defensive, with his majesty of Russia. The cry is, "all the Russians want is a fleet, and we'll lend them that." In fact, a deadly animosity pervades America towards Great Britain; and although it is not publicly confessed, for the Americans are too able politicians to do that, yet it is no less certain, that "*Delenda est Carthago*," is their motto. Let England look to it. Her power is great; but, if the fleets of America, France, and Russia, were to combine, and land on the shores of England hordes of Russians, and battalions of disciplined Frenchmen—if this were to be done, with the Irish people, instead of allies as they should be, her deadly enemies, her power is annihilated at a blow! For let it be remembered, that there is no rallying principle in the temperament of the mass of the English people; and that formerly one single victory,—the victory of Hastings, completely subjugated them. Hume, who was decidedly an impartial historian, is compelled to say of that conquest, "It would be difficult to find in all history a revolution more destructive, or attended with a more complete subjection of the ancient inhabitants. Contumely seems even to have been wantonly added to oppression; and the natives were universally reduced to such a state of meanness and poverty, that the English name became a term of reproach; and several generations elapsed before one family of Saxon pedigree was raised to any considerable honours, or could so much as obtain the rank of baron of the realm."—Yet the English people owe much to the ancestors of the aristocracy, who introduced among them the arts and refinements of civilization, and by their wisdom and disciplined valour have raised the country to that pitch of greatness, so justly termed "the envy of surrounding nations." I do not contend, that because a nation may have acquired the name of great, that therefore *the people* are more happy; but am rather inclined to think the contrary, for conquests are generally made and wealth is accumulated for the benefit of the few, and at the expense of the many.

A law has been lately passed by the legislature of Pennsylvania, taxing wholesale and retail dealers in merchandize, excepting those importers of foreign goods who vend the articles in the form in which they are imported. This act classes the citizens according to their annual amount of sales, and taxes them in the same proportion. Those who effect sales to the amount of fifty thousand dollars, constitute the first class; of forty thousand dollars, the second class; of thirty thousand dollars, the third class; of twenty thousand dollars, the fourth class; of fifteen thousand dollars, the fifth class; of ten thousand dollars, the sixth class; of five thousand dollars, the seventh class; and all persons effecting sales not exceeding two thousand five hundred dollars, constitute the eighth class. The first class shall pay for license, annually, fifty dollars; the second class, forty dollars; the third class, thirty dollars; the fourth class, twenty-five dollars; the fifth class, twenty dollars; the sixth class, fifteen dollars; the seventh class, twelve dollars and fifty cents, and the eighth class ten dollars.

Direct taxation has been found in all cases to be obnoxious, and this particular mode, I apprehend, is calculated to produce very pernicious effects. The laws of a republic should all tend to establish and support, as far as is practicable, the principle of equality, and any act that has a contrary tendency must be injurious to the community. Now this act draws a direct line of demarcation between citizens, in proportion to the extent of their dealings; and as in this country a man's importance is entirely estimated by his supposed wealth, the citizens of Pennsylvania can henceforth only claim a share of respectability, proportionate to the *class* to which they belong. The west country ladies have shewn a great aptitude for forming "circles of society," and the promulgation of this law affords them a most powerful aid in establishing a *store-keeping aristocracy.*

The large cities in America are by no means so lightly taxed as might be supposed from the cheapness of the government; the public works, public buildings, and police establishments, requiring adequate funds for their maintenance and support; however, the inhabitants have the consolation of knowing that this must gradually decrease, and that their money is laid out for their own advantage, and not for the purpose of pensioning off the mistresses and physicians of viceroys, as in Ireland.[23] Another thing is to be observed, that in addition to the *national* debt, each state has a *private* debt, which in many cases is tolerably large. These debts have been created by expenditures on roads, canals, and public buildings. The mode of taxation latterly adopted by the legislature is not popular, and many of the public prints have remonstrated against the system. "The Philadelphia Gazette," of the 24th Sept. 1830, makes the following remarks—"The subject of unequal and oppressive taxation deserves more attention than it has hitherto received from our citizens. The misery of England is occasioned less by the amount of revenue that is raised there, than by the manner in which it is raised. In Pennsylvania we are going on rapidly, making our state a second England in regard of debt and taxation. Our public debt is already 13,000,000 dollars; and before our canals and rail-roads shall be completed, it will probably amount to 18 or 20 millions. The law imposing taxes of 10, 20, 30, 40 and 50 dollars on retailers, is not the only just subject of complaint. The *collateral inheritance* tax is equally unjust. The tavern-keepers are besides to be taxed from 20 to 50 dollars each. Nor does the matter end here. At the next session of the legislature, it will, in all probability, be found necessary to lay on additional taxes: and when the principle of unjust taxation is once admitted in legislation, it is difficult to say how far it will be carried."

Whilst staying at Philadelphia an account of the French revolution arrived, and the merchants, there and at New York, were in high spirits, thinking that war was inevitable. A war in Europe is always hailed with delight in America, as it opens a field for commercial enterprise, and gives employment to the shipping, of which at present they are much in need.

During the long and ruinous war in Europe, the mercantile and shipping interests of the United States advanced with an unexampled degree of rapidity. The Americans were then the carriers of nearly all Europe, and scarcely any merchandize entered the ports of the belligerent powers, but in American bottoms. This unnatural state of prosperity could not last: peace was established, and from that era the decline of commerce in the United States may be dated. The merchants seem not to have calculated on this event's so soon taking place, or to have overrated the increase of prosperity and population in their own country, as up to that period, and for some years afterwards, there does appear to have been no relaxation of ship-building, and little diminution of mercantile speculations. At present the ship-owners are realizing little beyond the expenses of their vessels, and in many cases the bottoms are actually in debt. The frequent failures in the Atlantic cities, of late, are mainly to be attributed to unsuccessful ship speculations; and I am myself aware of more than one instance, where the freight was so extremely low, as to do little more than cover the expenditure of the voyage. On my return to Europe, while staying at Marseilles, twelve American vessels arrived in that port within the space of two months; and before my departure, nine of these returned to the United States with ballast (stones), and I believe only two with full cargos.

In a national point of view, the difficulty of obtaining employment for the shipping of America may not have been so injurious as at first view it appears to be; on the contrary, I am of opinion that it has been advantageous. Whilst a profitable trade could with facility be carried on with and in Europe, the merchants seldom thought of extending their enterprises to any other parts of the world; but since the decline of that trade, communications have been opened with the East Indies, Africa, all the ports of the Mediterranean, and voyages to the Pacific, and to the Austral regions, are now of common occurrence. The museums in the Atlantic cities bear ample testimony to the enterprising character of the American merchants, which by their means are filled with all the curious and interesting productions of the East. This has encouraged a taste for scientific studies, and for travelling; which must ultimately tend to raise the nation to a degree of respectability little inferior to the oldest European state.

FOOTNOTES:

[23]

An Irish viceroy lately paid his physician by conferring on him a baronetcy, and a pension of two hundred pounds a year, of the public money.

CHAPTER XI

Having sojourned for more than three weeks at Philadelphia, I departed for New York. The impressions made on my mind during that time were highly favourable to the Philadelphians and their city. It is the handsomest city in the Union; and the inhabitants, in sociability and politeness, have much the advantage of any other body of people with whom I came in contact.

The steamer takes you up the Delaware river to Bordentown, in New Jersey, twenty-four miles from Philadelphia. The country at either side is in a high state of cultivation. It is interspersed with handsome country seats, and on the whole presents a most charming prospect. There is scarcely a single point passed up the windings of the Delaware, but presents a new and pleasing variety of landscape—luxuriant foliage—gently swelling hills, and fertile lawns; which last having been lately mown, were covered with a rich green sward most pleasing to the eye. The banks of the river at Bordentown are high, and the town, as seen from the water, has a pretty effect. Here a stage took us across New Jersey to Amboy. This is not a large town, nor can it ever be of much importance, being situated too near the cities of New York and Philadelphia. At Amboy we again took the steam-boat up the bay, and after a delightful sail of thirty miles, through scenery the most beautiful and magnificent, we arrived at New York.

When I was at New York about fifteen months before, I was informed that the working classes were being organized into regular bodies, similar to the "union of trades" in England, for the purpose of retaining all political power in their own hands. This organization has taken place at the suggestion of Frances Wright, of whom I shall again have occasion to speak presently, and has succeeded to an astonishing extent. There are three or four different bodies of the "workies," as they call themselves familiarly, which vary somewhat from each other in their principles, and go different lengths in their attacks on the present institutions of society. There are those of them called "agrarians," who contend that there should be a law passed to prohibit individuals holding beyond a certain quantity of ground; and that at given intervals of time there should be an equal division of property throughout the land. This is the most ultra, and least numerous class; the absurdity of whose doctrines must ultimately destroy them as a body. Various handbills and placards may be seen posted about the city, calling meetings of these unions. Some of those handbills are of a most extraordinary character indeed. I shall here insert a copy of one, which I took off a wall, and have now in my possession. It may serve to illustrate the character of those clubs.

THE CAUSE OF THE POOR.

The Mechanics and other working men of the city of New York, and of *these* such and such only as live by their own useful industry, who wish to retain all political power in their own hands;

WHO ARE IN FAVOUR OF

A just compensation for labour,

Abolishing imprisonment for debt,

An efficient lien law,

A general system of education; including food, clothing and instruction, equal for all, at the public expense, *without separation of children from parents*,

Exemption from sale by execution, of mechanics' tools and implements sufficiently extensive to enable them to carry on business:

AND WHO ARE OPPOSED TO

Banks and Bankers,

Auctions and Auctioneers,

Monopolies and

Monopolists of all descriptions,

Brokers,

Lawyers, and

Rich men for office, and to all those, either rich or poor, who favour them,

Exemption of Property from Taxation:

Are invited to assemble at the Wooster-street Military Hall, on Thursday evening next, 16th Sept., at eight o'clock, to select by Ballot, from among the persons proposed on the 6th Instant, Candidates for Governor, Lieutenant-Governor, Senator, and a New Committee of Fifty, and to propose Candidates for Register, for Members of Congress, and for Assembly.

By order of the Committee of Fifty.

JOHN R. SOPER, *Chairman*. JOHN TUTHILL, *Secretary*.

So far for the "Workies;" and now for Miss Wright. If I understand this lady's principles correctly, they are strictly Epicurean. She contends, that mankind have nothing whatever to do with any but this tangible world;—that the sole and only legitimate pursuit of man, is terrestrial happiness;—that looking forward to an ideal state of existence, diverts his attention from the pleasures of this life—destroys all real sympathy towards his fellow-creatures, and renders him callous to their sufferings. However different the *theories* of other systems may be, she contends that the *practice* of the world, in all ages and generations, shews that this is the *effect* of their inculcation. These are alarming doctrines; and when this lady made her *debût* in public, the journals contended that their absurdity was too gross to be of any injury to society, and that in a few months, if she continued lecturing, it would be to empty benches.

The editor of "The New York Courier and Enquirer" and she have been in constant enmity, and have never failed denouncing each other when opportunity offered. Miss Wright sailed from New York for France, where she still remains, in the month of July, 1830; and previous to her departure delivered an address, on which "the New York Enquirer" makes the following observations:—

"The parting address of Miss Wright at the Bowery Theatre, on Wednesday evening, was a singular *melange* of politics and impiety—eloquence and irreligion—bold invective, and electioneering slang. The theatre was very much crowded, probably three thousand persons being present; and what was the most surprising circumstance of the whole, is the fact, that about *one half of the audience were females—respectable females.*

"When Fanny first made her appearance in this city as a lecturer on the 'new order of things,' she was very little visited by respectable females. At her first lecture in the Park Theatre, about half a dozen appeared; but these soon left the house. From that period till the present, we had not heard her speak in public; but her doctrines, and opinions, and philosophy, appear to have made much greater progress in the city than we ever dreamt of. Her fervid eloquence—her fine action—her *soprano-toned* voice—her bold and daring attacks upon all the present systems of society—and particularly upon priests, politicians, bankers, and aristocrats as she calls them, have raised a party around her of considerable magnitude, and of much fervour and enthusiasm."

"The present state of things in this city is, to say the least of it, very singular. A bold and eloquent woman lays siege to the very foundations of society—inflames and excites the public mind—declaims with vehemence against every thing religious and orderly, and directs the whole of her movements to accomplish the election of a ticket next fall, under the title of the 'working-man's ticket.'[24] She avows that her object is a thorough and radical reform and change in every relation of life—even the dearest and most sacred. Father, mother, husband, wife, son, and daughter, in all their delicate and endearing relationships, are to be swept away equally with clergymen, churches, banks, parties, and benevolent societies. Hundreds and hundreds of respectable families, by frequenting her lectures, give countenance and currency to these startling principles and doctrines. Nearly the whole newspaper press of the city maintain a death-like silence, while the great Red Harlot of Infidelity is madly and triumphantly stalking over the city, under the mantle of 'working-men,' and making *rapid progress* in her work of ruin. If a solitary newspaper raise a word in favour of public virtue and private morals, in defence of the rights, liberties, and property of the community, it is denounced with open bitterness by some, and secretly stabbed at by them who wish to pass for good citizens. Miss Wright says she leaves the city soon. This is a mere *ruse* to call her followers around her. The effect of her lectures is already boasted of by her followers. 'Two years ago,' say they,—'*twenty persons* could scarcely be found in New York who would openly avow infidelity—now we have *twenty thousand.*—Is not that something?'

"We say it is something—something that will make the whole city think."

On the day of my departure for Europe, is was announced to the merchants of New York, that the West India ports were opened to American vessels.

This is a heavy blow to the interests of the British colonies; and it does not appear that even Great Britain *herself* has received any equivalent for inflicting so serious an injury on a portion of the empire by no means unimportant. The Canadians and Nova Scotians found a market for their surplus produce in the West Indies, for which they took in return the productions of these islands—thus a reciprocal advantage was derived to the sister colonies. But now, from the proximity of the West Indies to the Atlantic cities of the United States, American produce will be poured into these markets, for which, in return, little else than specie will be brought back to the ports of the Republic.

It may be said, that an equivalent has been obtained by the removal of restrictions hitherto laid on British shipping. This I deny is any thing like an equivalent, as the trade with America is carried on almost exclusively in American bottoms. I particularly noted at New Orleans, Baltimore, Philadelphia, and New York, the paucity of British vessels in those ports; and ascertained that it was the practice among American merchants, who it must be observed are nearly all extensive ship-owners, to withhold cargos, even at some inconvenience, from foreign vessels, and await the arrival of those of their own country. I do not positively assert that the ships of *any other* nation are preferred to those of England; but, as far as my personal observations on that point have gone, I am strongly inclined to think that such is the fact.

The mercantile and shipping interests of Great Britain must continue to decline, if the government suffers itself continually to be cajoled into measures of this nature, and effects treaties the advantages of which appear to be all on one side, and in lieu of its concessions receives no just equivalent; unless a little empty praise for "liberal policy" and "generosity," can be so termed. I am well aware that it may have been of some small advantage to the West Indies to be enabled to obtain their supplies from the United States; but with reference to the policy of the measure, I speak only of the empire at large. Nearly all the Canadians with whom I conversed, freely acknowledged that they have not shaken off the yoke of England, only because they enjoyed some advantages by their connexion with her: but as these are diminished, the ties become loosened, and at length will be found too weak to hold them any longer. Disputes have already arisen between the people and the government relative to church lands, which appropriations they contend are unjust and dishonest.

No doubt the question of tariff duties on the raw material imported into England, is one of great delicacy as connected with the manufacturing interests of the country; yet it does appear to me, that a small duty might without injury be imposed on American cottons *imported in American bottoms.* This would afford considerable encouragement to the shipping of Great Britain and her colonies, and could by no means be injurious to the manufacturing interests. The cottons of the Levant have been latterly increasing in quantity, and a measure of this nature would be likely to promote their further and rapid increase; which is desirable, as it would leave us less dependent on America, than we now are, for the raw material. The shipping of America is not held by the cotton-growing states; and although the nationality of the southerns is no doubt great, yet their love of self-interest is much greater, and would always preponderate in their choice of vessels. It would be even better, if found necessary, to make some arrangement in the shape of draw-back, than that a nation which has imposed a duty on our manufactured goods, almost amounting to a prohibition, should reap so much advantage from our system of "liberal and generous" policy. I shall conclude these *rambling* sketches by observing, that there are two things eminently remarkable in America: the one is, that every American from the highest to the lowest, thinks the Republican form of government *the best;* and the other, that the seditious and rebellious of all countries become there the most peaceable and contented citizens.

We sailed from New York on the 1st of October, 1830. The monotony of a sea voyage, with unscientific people, is tiresome beyond description. The journal of a single day is the history of a month. You rise in the morning, and having performed the necessary ablutions, mount on deck,—"Well Captain, how does she head?"—"South-east by east"—(our course is east by south).—"Bad, bad, Captain—two points off." You then promenade the quarter-deck, until the black steward arrests your progress—grins in your face, and announces breakfast. Down you go, and fall foul of ham, beef, *pommes de terre frites*, jonny-cakes, and *café sans lait;* and generally, in despite of bad cooking and occasional lee-lurches, contrive to eat an enormous meal. Breakfast being despatched, you again go on deck—promenade—gaze on the clouds—then read a little, if perchance you have books with you—lean over the gunwale, watching the waves and the motion of the vessel; but the eternal water, clouds, and sky—sky, clouds, and water, produce a listlessness that nothing can overcome. In the Atlantic, a ship in sight is an object which arouses the attention of all on board—to speak one is an æra, and furnishes to the captain and mates a subject for the day's conversation. Thus situated, an occasional spell of squally weather is by no means uninteresting:—the lowering aspect of the sky—the foaming surges, which come rolling on, threatening to overwhelm the tall ship, and bury her in the fathomless abyss of the ocean—the laugh of the gallant tars, when a sea sweeps the deck and drenches them to the skin—all these incidents, united, rather amuse the voyager, and tend to dispel the inanity with which he is afflicted. During these periods, I have been for hours watching the motions of the "stormy petrel" (*procellaria pelagica*), called by sailors, "mother Carey's chickens." These birds are seldom seen in calm weather, but appear to follow the gale, and when it blows most heavily they are seen in greatest numbers. The colour is brown and white; the size about that of the swallow, whose motions oh the wing they resemble. They skim over the surface of the roughest sea, gliding up and down the undulations with astonishing swiftness. When they observe their prey, they descend flutteringly, and place the feet and the tips of the wings on the surface of the water. In this position I have seen many of them rest for five or six seconds, until they had completed the capture. The petrel is to be seen in all parts of the Atlantic, no matter how distant from land; and the oldest seaman with whom I have conversed on the subject, never saw one of them rest. Humboldt says, that in the Northern Deserta, the petrels hide in rabbit burrows.

A few days' sail brought us into the "Gulf stream," the influence of which is felt as high as the 43° north latitude. We saw a considerable quantity of *fucus natans*, or gulf weed, but it generally was so far from the vessel, that I could not contrive to procure a sprig. Mr. Luccock, in his Notes on Brazil, says, that "if a nodule of this weed, taken fresh from the water at night, is hung up in a small cabin, it emits phosphorescent light enough to render objects visible." He describes the leaves of this plant as springing from the joints of the branches, oblong, indented at the edges, about an inch and a half long, and a quarter of an inch broad. Humboldt's description is somewhat different: he calls it the "vine-leaved fucus;" says, "the leaves are circular, of a *tender* green, and indented at the edges, stem brown, and three inches long."—What I saw of this weed rather agrees with that described by Humboldt—the leaves were shaped like the vine leaf, and of a rusty-green colour. That portion of the Atlantic between the 22d and 34th parallels of latitude, and 26th and 58th meridians of longitude, is generally covered with fuci, and is termed by the Portuguese, *mar do sargasso*, or grassy sea. It was supposed by many, from the large quantities of this weed seen in the Gulf stream, that it grew on the Florida rocks, and by the influence and extension of the current, was detached and carried into this part of the Atlantic. However, this position is not tenable, as a single branch of fucus has never been found on the Florida reef. Humboldt, and other scientific men, are of opinion that this weed vegetates at the bottom of the ocean—that being detached from its root, it rises to the surface; and that such portion of it as is found in the stream, is drawn thither by the sweeping of the current along the edge of the weedy sea. Moreover, the fuci that are found in the northern extremity of the Florida stream are generally decayed, while those which are seen in the southern extremity appear quite fresh—this difference would not exist if they emanated from the Gulf.

We stood to the north of the Azores, with rather unfavourable winds, and at length came between the coast of Africa and Cape St. Vincent. Here we had a dead calm for four entire days. The sky was perfectly cloudless, and the surface of the ocean was like oil. Not being able to do better, we got out the boat and went turtle fishing, or rather catching, in company with a very fine shark, which thought proper to attend us during our excursion. In such weather the turtles come to the surface of the water to sleep and enjoy the solar heat, and if you can approach without waking them, they fall an easy prey, being rendered incapable of resistance by their shelly armour. We took six. Attached to the breast of one was a remora, or "sucking fish." The length of this animal is from six to eight inches—colour blackish—body, scaleless and oily—head rather flat, on the back of which is the sucker, which consists of a narrow oval-shaped margin with several transverse projections, and ten curved rays extending towards the centre, but not meeting. The Indians of Jamaica and Cuba employed this fish as falconers do hawks. In calm weather, they carried out those which they had kept and fed for the purpose, in their canoes, and when they had got to a sufficient distance, attached the remora to the head of the canoe by a strong line of considerable length. When the remora perceives a fish, which he can do at a considerable distance, he darts away with astonishing rapidity, and fastens upon it. The Indian lets go the line, to which a buoy is attached to mark the course the remora has taken, and follows in his canoe until he thinks the game is exhausted; he then draws it gradually in, the remora still adhering to his prey. Oviedo says, "I have known a turtle caught by this method, of a bulk and weight which no single man could support."

For four days we were anxiously watching for some indications of a breeze, but were so frequently deceived with "cat's paws," and the occasional slight flickering of the dog vane, that we sank into listless resignation. At length our canvass filled, and we soon came within sight of the Straits of Gibraltar. On our left was the coast of Spain, with its vineyards and white villages; and on our right lay the sterile hills of Barbary. Opposite Cape Trafalgar is Cape Spartel, a bold promontory, on the west side of which is a range of basaltic pillars. The entrance to the Mediterranean by the Straits, when the wind is unfavourable, is extremely difficult; but to pass out is almost impossible, the current continually setting in through the centre of the passage. Hence, onwards, the sail was extremely pleasant, being within sight of the Spanish coast, and the Islands of Yvica, Majorca, and Minorca, successively, until we reached the Gulf of Lyons. When the northerly wind blows, which, in Provence, is termed the *mistral*, the waves roll against the coast of Provence, and the recoil produces that ugly chopping sea for which this gulf is renowned. In the Mediterranean, even in the calmest weather, a light pleasant breeze springs up after sunset; this and the cloudless sky, and unobscured brilliancy of the stars, are attractions sufficient to allure the most somnolent and unromantic mortal to remain on deck.

The molusca, or oceanic insect, which emits a phosphorescent light, appeared here in vast quantities, which induced me to try experiments. I took a piece of black crape, and having folded it several times, poured some sea water taken fresh in a bucket, upon it: the water in the bucket, when agitated by the hand, gave out sparkling light. When the crape was thoroughly saturated with water, I took it to a dark part of the cabin, when it seemed to be studded with small sparkling stars; but more of the animals I could not then discern. Next day I put some water in a glass tumbler, and having exposed it to a strong solar light, with the help of a magnifying glass was enabled distinctly to discern the moluscæ. When magnified, they appeared about the size of a pin's head, of a yellowish brown colour, rather oval-shaped, and having tentaculæ. The medusa is a genus of molusca; and I think M. le Seur told me he reckons forty-three or forty-four species of that genus.

We crossed the Gulf of Lyons, and came within the road of Marseilles, where we were taken charge of by a pilot. When we reached the mouth of the basin, a boat came alongside of us, and a man handed up a piece of wood, and said, "Mettez sur cela le nom du capitaine et du batiment;"—we were to perform quarantine. Whoever has performed quarantine can commiserate our condition. No one can quit the quarantine ground, or rather the space in the harbour alloted to vessels performing quarantine. If it be necessary to send any papers from the ship on shore, they are taken with a forceps and plunged into vinegar. If the sails of any other vessel touch those of one in quarantine, she too must undergo several days' probation. Our time was five days; but as we had clean bills of health, and had lost none of our crew on the passage, we were allowed to count the day of our entering and the day of our going out of quarantine. The usual ceremonies being performed, I again stepped on European ground, and felt myself at home.

Lightning Source UK Ltd.
Milton Keynes UK
UKHW040036170123
415467UK00003B/91

9 783752 360325